Rider Out of Yesterday

Dallas Marchant was the only man to escape from a hellish Mexican prison and survive. But when he returned to Texas he found that things had changed a great deal in the eight years he'd been gone.

There was no wife, no ranch and no land. Even the guns were different. But he had had to fight all his life for everything so it was no real surprise when he had to start fighting for what was rightfully his – even if it meant taking on the biggest and most ruthless cattle baron in Comanche County.

Rider Out of Yesterday

JAKE DOUGLAS

A Black Horse Western

ROBERT HALE · LONDON

© Jake Douglas 2004
First published in Great Britain 2004

ISBN 0 7090 7563 4

Robert Hale Limited
Clerkenwell House
Clerkenwell Green
London EC1R 0HT

Typeset by
Derek Doyle & Associates, Liverpool.
Printed and bound in Great Britain by
Antony Rowe Limited, Wiltshire

CHAPTER 1

BLACK HELL

There were six of them making the attempted break-out but they figured that, at best, only one of them might make it out alive.

Dallas Marchant had no notion that he might be the one eventually to reach freedom after seven years in this place they called *el Inferno Negro* – the Black Hell.

It was a move full of desperation, near-panic and not a little resolve. Some said, even suicide thrown in . . . There were four of the original ten gringos still surviving and the Mexican brothers, Ignacio and Raul, had joined them because, should any of them survive the attempt, these two knew their own country best. The night before the date of the break-out they drew each man a crude map on scraps of leather and some greasy bits of paper. The charcoal they used smudged and the maps were far from accurate but they were all that was available.

Hansen, now like a living skeleton, dropped beside Marchant during the one short ten-minute break they were allowed in the quarry. He was filthy, scabbed, one eye hooded permanently and with a broken rib that would never heal – not if the guard they called the Bull had anything to do with it.

'Ready for it?'

Marchant, his gaunt face bearded with dirt-clogged curly hair, moved only his deep-set eyes towards the man he had ridden down from Texas with all those years ago. They had been young and laughing and full of sap and a sense of adventure then, aiming to cut into the great longhorn herds of Don Renaldo, drive them back to Texas, split with the others and each man use the grass-fat cattle to start his own herd on prove-up land.

Marchant snorted: now here they were, two men old before their time, half-crippled, no meat nor sinew nor muscle worthy of the name on their ill-fed bodies. And yet they were going to try the impossible: escape from the Black Hell.

To where. . . ?

That was what it had come down to: to stay meant eventual death. To escape – or try to – meant the same thing. And if, by some miracle they were successful, what awaited them beyond the walls. . . ?

The 'Hell' part was still out there, sun that blasted the earth itself to desiccated dust and crumbling rocks, that would blind a man, flay the hide from his bones. It sucked up water the instant it appeared whether it be by way of dew, a rare shower of rain, a spring bursting through – or spilled from a saddle canteen grown too hot to hold.

What would they live on? There were only snakes and lizards out in that furnace country, some beetles, maybe. Even the scattered cactus looked shrivelled. A man could be blinded by that glare and wander in circles until he simply dropped and fried where he fell.

There would be no pursuit to speak of once they were out of sight of the look-out towers – the *commandante* knew better than to expend his men's energies chasing down anyone fool enough to try to escape his prison. Let the Devil take care of them – in twenty years Old Nick had never let the *commandante* down.

Yet, knowing that all this, and worse, awaited them, Marchant somehow worked up a crooked grin that allowed his chipped and gapped teeth to flash briefly as he winked at Hansen.

'Ready!' he grated.

Then the Bull was amongst the resting men, slashing with his whip, kicking with his heavy boots and raking with his spurs.

'Back to work, my beauties! There is a whole mountain for you to reduce to rubble yet! – *Prisa! Prisa, canalla!*'

Words the convicts had been hearing day after day for all the years the Bull had been in charge of the quarry detail.

'Hurry! Hurry, you scum!'

Always followed by the lash of his whip or a slash with the nobbly length of bamboo he sometimes preferred.

Yeah! Marchant thought as he lifted his heavy

sledge. *He was ready – Whatever waited beyond those walls had to be better than this!*

Once the head-count at sundown used to be taken in the large courtyard, the shuffling, staggering, moaning prisoners assembled, pushed and shoved by the guards into some form of line, and then other guards would walk amongst them, touching each man as they went, counting.

But when the count was wrong – and, surprisingly, this happened more frequently than might be expected – there was chaos and delays and tempers grew short and clubs swung and men were injured or worse and work-time was lost. So the *commandante* decreed that the men would be herded into their shedlike dormitories and two guards with them would be responsible for the correct count of heads. If there was a wrong count, then that meant only the fifty men in one shed would be involved instead of the whole prison community. It worked well enough although if a man was missing, temporarily or otherwise for some reason, the men in the hut soon learned they could cover for the absence simply by shuffling around and confusing the guards who only wanted to lock them down and get to their supper anyway.

Tonight, the count would be down in Hut 9. By six. And those who were not going were of such desperate morale that they were willing to cover for the absences and risk the wrath of the *commandante*. Such an escape attempt took much courage and few could find the resolve to even plan for such an event. So those involved were respected, almost revered – not envied, because everyone was convinced they were going to their deaths. Yet that in itself was probably the surest and best escape of all from this hellish place. . . .

The six were in a group – Marchant, Hansen, Ignacio, Rant, Pedder and Castle. One of the guards doing the counting tonight was the Bull.

The temptation was too much for Hansen who had suffered most from the Bull's brutality. They faced each other, nose to nose, the big, flat-faced Mexican slowly smiling.

'*Amigo!*' he greeted suddenly, expansively. 'You are out of position, no? Your line should be two more back beside – *Ah!* Dallas – you, too, are out of – position . . .' His words slowed as his eyes squinted and his devious mind sensed that there could be a reason for this. No prisoner changed his position on the first count without risking punishment. Yet, now that he looked again, here were *six* men in the wrong line. Four gringos, and the Mexican Alvarez brothers.

Something strange here. . . .

The Bull started to step back, a hand dropping to the polished hilt of the club that swung at his side in its leather thong.

'I – think – I – don't like – this!'

'Then you won't like this even more!'

Hansen stepped after him and the short knife he had laboriously made over a four-month period from a broken rock chisel flashed dully in the smoky lanternlight and was buried to the hilt in the Bull's thick belly. Warm blood spurted over Hansen's hand even as the men about him began to scatter, unprepared for this move. The Bull was so startled that he didn't scream or cry out. He looked down in utter astonishment as the knife turned and twisted in his corrupt body, raised his widening eyes to Hansen's taut face. The gringo withdrew the blade, stabbed again. Then the Alvarez brothers stepped in and their knives flashed, too, burying their steel in the Bull. The big guard sagged to his knees as the knives drove in and out, in and out. The second guard, busy counting on the far side, became aware of some disturbance, called the Bull's name, then, a mite apprehensively, drew his club and started shouldering his way through the men who crowded close, hindering him.

He began to shout and Marchant called:

'Shut him up!' The guard went down under a hail of bony fists and stomping, leathery, calloused feet, the prisoners tearing his clothes from him. There were no weapons except the clubs – guards were prohibited from carrying guns or knives inside any of the huts.

By now the Bull was dead in a welter of blood and Dallas placed a hand on Hansen's skeletal shoulder. The man's head snapped around, sunken eyes burning with a new madness, skin drawn skull-like over his wild face.

'Time to go, Kyle,' Marchant said quietly and saw the blood lust slowly fade from the other's eyes. Hansen nodded as Dallas raised his arms and with the others' help settled down the prisoners who were staring in horror at what had been done. 'Blame us – *we* killed the guards. We had weapons. You couldn't stop us. We killed them and then left . . . There will be punishment, you can expect that, but keep saying we did the killings and it won't be too bad. Now – *adios!*

They moved swiftly. They had rehearsed often enough and it went smoothly. The flagstones were quickly removed at the far end of the hut. They dropped down into the hole one by one. Candles were lit as the flagstones were replaced above them and the smell of the earth was all round them.

It had taken them a year and a half to dig this tunnel and they had lost three men during that time to cave-ins and suffocation.

They had learned about ventilaton and shoring up the walls as they went along, progressing slowly, sometimes no more than a foot a week if guard activity or accidents prevented it. But the tunnel had been completed – its exit was outside the western wall, the one with the overhang so that a small patch of ground was obscured from the guards in the lookout tower above. They were lazy men, anyway – here hadn't been an escape attempt in three years. . . .

This one looked like being successful.

Choking in the heated air despite the cleverly concealed ventilation shafts, they crawled through, Hansen leading, followed by Ignacio, then Castle, Raul, Dallas and finally Pedder.

The exit hole had yet to be dug. The best of their crude shovels was waiting and fresh candles were lit. Hansen, kneeling, scraped at the crumbling earth, cursing as clods fell upon him, clogging his hair and mouth, filling his torn shirt. The men were all breathing hard now, gasping, sweating, urging him to hurry.

Then there was a virtual cascade of dirt mixed with a few strands of half-dead grass – and a flood of night air.

'I see – stars!' choked Hansen, and stifled the urge to laugh hysterically, clawing the hole wider than his bony shoulders, boosted up by Ignacio. 'Ah, God, Dallas! That – air – tastes – mighty good!'

They tended to crush in upon one another but there was enough discipline for Hansen and Ignacio to kneel by the hole they had opened and help the others up. Dallas allowed Pedder to go before him, staying to extinguish the last candle so its glow would not attract any guard who was more alert than usual.

Above, the men were just starting to break for the nearest clump of cactus and Dallas had his arms over the side of the hole, Castle reaching down to help him, when his blood froze.

'*Bienvenido, amigos!* We have been expecting you!'

God almighty! That was the *commandante*'s voice!

Castle had been squatting and now fell backwards in shock, Dallas half-in, half-out of the hole.

Shadows moved out of the clump of cactus – starlight streaking along the barrels of the long Snider rifles issued to the prison guards. Dull light also flashed from the polished leather belt and holster and medals of the prison commander as he waved his big Le Mat revolver, spreading out his men.

'*Matar! Asesinar!*'

The commander's orders were short and clear –

12

Kill them! Murder them!

The rifles fired, bolts working swiftly, shot after shot cutting into the stunned escapees. Hansen went down with four bullets tearing apart his thin body. Ignacio's face exploded into bone and pieces of bloody flesh. Raul's throat was torn out and his blood-gush hosed Pedder who reared up, clawing at his face while his body danced and jerked with the thud of hammering lead. Castle tried to leap up but was cut down by the *commandante*'s revolver and his body fell across Dallas's shoulders as the man flung himself out of the hole, knowing that to go back into the tunnel was sure suicide.

But lead found him. Tore up his back in a long gash, blood flowing copiously. A second shot clipped his head and blood poured down across his face. Then sand stung him as other bullets drove into the ground where he lay and, working by instinct through the pain that washed over him, he crawled under Castle and the twitching Pedder.

The sounds of crashing gunfire faded away into the desert night and the *commandante* called for lanterns. The guards walked amongst the corpses, kicking them apart, separating them. Dallas felt a hard boot tear skin from over his ribs, somehow managed to stifle the grunt of pain, forced himself to flop loosely on to his side, scarcely breathing.

He felt the heat from a lantern held close to his face, knew the light would be reflected from the mask of blood covering one side of his face.

'All dead, *commandante*,' a rough voice above him reported.

'A good hour's work.' The guards relaxed at the pleased tone of their leader's words. They knew their lives, as much as those of the prisoners, hung on this madman's moods. 'Send someone to warn my chef to lay out my supper . . . .'

'*Sí Commandante!*' The orders were given and as the officer made to move away, the guard asked: 'Shall we get a burial detail, *Commandante*?'

The man paused briefly.

'No. Leave them for the coyotes. It is a long time since we have fed our friends of the desert. If there is anything left by daylight, shovel it into the tunnel and seal it off.' His voice hardened. 'And that is the last I wish to hear of this affair until morning.'

'Er . . . the man who betrayed them. . . ?'

The Le Mat revolver suddenly roared and the guard was blown off his feet. The *commandante* scowled at the startled soldiers.

'Leave him for the coyotes, also. He does not listen to what I say!' He holstered the pistol, started to turn away and then snapped, 'The man who betrayed this scum shall be rewarded. Fifty lashes should be adequate. If he lives, you may double his rations for one week. Now, I go to table.'

The soldiers hurriedly stepped aside, except one man who ran on ahead to open the Judas-gate in the main portal to *el Inferno Negro* for the *commandante*.

CHAPTER 2

SURVIVOR

Although it was the end of winter and a few days into the official spring, it was cold up here on the high plains. There was a wind that seemed gentle and balmy enough down on the flats but up here it tended to cut through a man's clothing and rattle his ribs for him.

Dallas sprawled, forcing his long body down into the small crevice between the barely warmed rocks, and adjusted the field glasses.

He picked up two riders in the field of vision, coming, as instructed, around the north-west side of the butte, from the direction of Daybright's Top D. They rode casually but with plenty of confidence, and as they started down the trail to the Lindon spread, he swung the glasses until he could see the log cabin and the surrounding area.

Corey Lindon wasn't much of a builder, but then he was a greenhorn, coming from somewhere out of one of the big Eastern states according to Dallas's information. A greenhorn but a man willing and eager to learn and with a streak of stubbornness in him that was going to cost him some teeth and hide, if not, eventually, his life. He was of medium build and worked now on a rail fence around what was obviously going to be a vegetable patch. Lindon's wife, Jemma, a small, huddled figure, was crouched by a turned-over garden-bed, planting seedlings. Smoke rose lazily from the chimney. Birds were resting on the roof-line of the partly completed barn.

A nice, pioneeering scene in the crisp bright sunlight.

It was about to be disrupted by the two riders who had reached the bottom of the trail now and were splashing their mounts across the shallow creek. It seemed that neither Corey nor Jemma Lindon had heard their approach and went on about their chores.

Dallas slid back, standing only when he was below the crest where he had a patient grey gelding waiting. The weight of the new model Colt Peacemaker felt strange on his right hip. For about the twentieth time he told himself he must try it slung butt-foremost on his left side, the way he used to wear the old Navy Colt which, along with the battered Henry repeater he had taken from a Yankee he had killed on the last day of the War, had once been his main armament in those wild years after Appomattox.

Now he had the new-fangled Peacemaker, a cartridge weapon, single-action, the deadliest and most popular pistol in the world at that time. And a brass-actioned '66 Winchester, both shooting .44/.40

calibre, making it necessary for a man to carry only one type of ammunition.

Things had sure changed in the seven years he had spent in the Black Hell – and the ten months after making it out alive across that inferno of a desert.

He swung aboard the grey and, as he picked his way down towards a back trail that would lead him up behind the Lindon spread, he once more thought about that miraculous escape of his. . . .

Left for dead with the corpses of the others and the guard shot by the *commandante* outside the wall of the prison, he had come round to hear the growling of animals – and feel the pressure of hungry canine teeth in his left ankle. Instinctive, sub-conscious fear had sent the adrenaline pumping through him and he had come out of his daze, kicking and fighting. His violent movements must have startled the coyote for it yelped and backed off, cringing in the night. Then it bared its fangs again and lunged back, others of the pack already working on the scattered bodies.

Dallas Marchant had the dead guard's legs across his lower body. He kicked the man's corpse at the coyote and heard the rattle of the guard's club against stone. He lunged after it, tore it from the leather belt-loop and turned in time to crush the skull of the coyote that closed in on him. Something warm splashed into his face and across his hands. The dog fell, twitching. Its companions were busy feasting, snarling at each other. Shaking, sticky blood half-blinding him in one eye, he felt feverishly over the guard's body. *Had the others left his weapons? His pistol, or knife. . . ?*

The gun was gone, but the belt-knife was there. On all fours, mouth parched with fear that the other dogs might turn their attention to him, Dallas took the man's belt and knife, buckled it about his skinny body. It sagged, too large, but it would do. He spun and stumbled as a dark hairy shape lunged for his throat. The whistling hardwood club connected with that supple, rib-straked body in mid-air.

The animal yelped, fell. He stomped on it with his leather-hard bare feet, feeling the pain in his left ankle where the first dog had bitten him. He smashed at the slavering jaws and felt bone break. Again, and this time he crushed the skull, and then he was lurching and staggering away into the clump of cactus.

Near exhaustion, pain across his back from the bullet wound, he collapsed to his hands and knees, a death-grip on the club, head hanging, gagging for breath. One of the bored guards on the wall might be trying to see the bloody feast but most likely had seen plenty in the past and wouldn't bother.

The coyote pack were going to be busy for quite a while yet. He had to be long gone by the time they were finished, though they likely wouldn't come after him until they were hungry again.

But he had to find cover before daylight: a man could see for many miles across that hellish country from the top of the prison lookout tower. . . .

It had all been a blur after the fight with the coyote. He had discovered that he had two more dog-bites, one in his right forearm, the other above the right knee. They slowed him down and his general debilitated condition didn't help. He had flashes of staggering and stumbling through darkness, stars blazing in the clear air, crawling, falling full length, pulling himself along on scraped elbows and knees, still with that death-grip on the bloodstained club. His throat was swollen, his tongue filling his mouth. He could see only out of one eye. The top of his head felt as if it was ready to blow off. His lungs burned and strained for air, which was hot and abrasive, stirred up by his own movements.

Twice he found himself crawling during daylight: *must be loco,* he thought once – he remembered that clearly.

He also remembered rolling on to his back and, almost blinded by the searing orb of the high sun, seeing something come between him and that murderous star. Just a shapeless shadow. Then something grabbed him like a steel claw around the throat and red and white lights streaked behind his eyes and he thought, *This is it! I'm going – I'm dying. . . .*

But he lived. There were Mimbreno Apaches in this part of the country, holed up in the sierras, venturing down into the desert on their mysterious missions from time to time, men who knew where there were hidden springs, even if a man had to strain the dead insects from the sluggish water with his teeth. But they knew it was life and their bellies had long ago become used to the filthy bacteria they also ingested. Living in the Black Hell, Marchant's belly had had to grow used to all kinds of filth and that was what allowed him to survive drinking the foul water given him.

These were Apaches on the run, some with their homes in Texas or Arizona. White men and Mexicans hunted them for their scalps, even slaughtering their children, sewing the smaller scalps together to form an adult-size so they could claim a bigger bounty. These Indians hated white men but they hated Mexicans still more. The ones who had found Dallas recognized the rotting, drab mustard-coloured clothing he wore as the 'uniform' of the condemned ones in *el Inferno Negro*.

It was what saved him. If they could take a man away from the hated Mexicans, then to the Indian way of thinking, it was a victory worthy of celebration.

Six months Dallas had spent with the sierra fugitives and, slowly recovering from his years of ill-treatment in the prison, he had only just managed to escape a raid on their camp by bounty hunters. He had jumped a white man in a Texas saddle, driving his knife to the hilt between the man's shoulders, kicking the body from the prancing horse. As the corpse rolled away, Dallas snatched at the man's pistol butt, felt it wrench free of the holster and, for the first time in his life held one of the Colt Peacemakers that were revolutionizing the entire frontier lands.

He had always been a man who knew his firearms and it took him only seconds to discover that although the gun was heavier than the Navy Colt it was well-balanced, and a man still only had to thumb back the hammer and pull the trigger in order to shoot it.

He thrust it into the snarling face of a Mexican rider with perhaps a dozen Indian scalps on his saddle horn, dropped the hammer and blew the man out of the saddle. He twisted fast at the sound of a curse and the thunder of hoofs, blasted a white man out of the saddle, wrenched his fighting horse aside, but not fast enough. The other animal crashed into his mount and they went down, thrashing and kicking. Dallas rolled away, came up on one knee in an instinctive move learned long ago during the War, and chopped at the hammer spur with the edge of his hand. He shot down a rider and horse together, turned at a yell, saw one of the Indians leading a riderless mount, and vaulted into the saddle.

Everything was blurred after that. The smoking Peacemaker was soon empty and he thrust the gun into his waistband, following the Indians through fighting, swearing men, guns thundering deafeningly in his ears. They rode away from the burning village and the wails of the women and children who still lived, even as more bounty hunters swept in from the other side. There was nothing they could do. . . .

Eventually he made it back to Texas and by then he had his Winchester and a holster rig for the Peacemaker with ample ammunition. He had no money so he had to steal what he wanted, but he had been stealing for years before he had ridden down to Mexico with Hansen's bunch and into disaster. . . .

Now he was back. And had learned the hard way that things were not going to go as planned.

Carrie was gone for one thing, though that was no surprise, and he didn't blame her. Starry-eyed, she had watched him ride out at sundown that fateful night eight years ago, already half-drunk on

21

Hansen's Tennessee moonshine, heading for glory and riches. She hadn't looked convinced, but she hadn't tried very hard to stop him. She knew he was right: if they could gather Mexican cattle from one of the huge *ranchos* just south of the Rio, it would set them up, well along the way to proving-up on their quarter-section.

His luck had run out – and so had Carrie it seemed. It took him three months to track her down. She was living in New Mexico, in a small town where she worked in a bakery – she had always been a fine cook.

She didn't recognize him: the Black Hell had wrought too many changes in the laughing, tow-headed rakehell of a cowpoke she had married and tried to build a home with. She had remarried after years of hearing nothing of him, the quarter-section long gone to someone else. She was bitter at first but relented a little after a while.

'Well, I did warn you that one of your crazy schemes would backfire badly one day, Dal.'

He nodded, gaunt face looking stern and ... deadly, almost, with that bullet scar above his left eye which caused the outer lid to hood a little.

'I've learned my lesson, Carrie ...'

'I doubt it. What're you going to do?'

He shrugged. She had been widowed, and there were no kids. She seemed content with her dreary life: possibly it was because it was in direct contrast to the wild times she had shared with him in the old days.

'You're a man out of yesterday, Dal. You look very

different, but I'll bet you haven't yet really grown up.'

'Mebbe. Think I'll go back to Texas. This . . . Tag Daybright, who took over our section – what's he like?'

She frowned. 'I don't really know. He owns a lot more land than we had, I do know that. And there are rumours that he hasn't always acquired it . . . legally.'

'Uh-huh. Might go look him up.'

She snapped her gaze at him.

'Why? What've you got in mind?'

He spread his hands. 'Work, I guess.'

She shook her head, the thick brown hair coming loose briefly and spilling about her pale face.

'You still lie to me – when it suits you.'

'If I lied to you before, it was only to protect you, Carrie.'

'What does that mean?'

He smiled, on-off. 'Whatever you want it to. Maybe I'll stop by again.' He was making for the door of her small rented cabin as he spoke.

'Don't bother, Dal. I – I like to think I'm over you now. And I'd prefer to keep it that way.'

Hand resting on the door latch, his beard-shagged face was sober as he asked:

'This second husband. He treat you all right?'

She stiffened. 'It's water under the bridge. Goodbye, Dallas.'

He went, but he spent a little more time in town and learned that the man she had married had been a heavy drinker and had knocked her about badly. One day he turned up dead in the garbage pit behind their house. It was generally thought that, drunk, he staggered in and fell face down and suffocated. But there were also rumours that there was an unexplained lump with deep bruising and a cut on the back of his head.

As he rode out of town, Dallas Marchant smiled thinly. 'Serve the bastard right,' he said, half aloud, and gave a mock salute in the direction of Carrie's cabin where she was hanging out some washing.

She gave no sign she had seen him.

He rode all the way back to Texas into the high plains, and asked Tag Daybright for a job.

Daybright was a big man, moved easily, smoked slim cigarillos and dressed slovenly for a man who was reportedly the richest in the county. He didn't seem very friendly and he had two hard-eyed ranch hands standing by as Dallas stood at the bottom of the porch steps and told the rancher his experience with cattle.

'Don't sound no better'n the average cowpoke,' Daybright said, puffing at his cigarillo. 'Why should I hire you when I got a dozen just as good or better already?'

'Figured maybe you could always use an extra top hand . . . who can take care of himself.'

Daybright smiled crookedly, not an unhandsome man, but with fleshy lips that peeled tightly back from even white teeth, making it more like an animal's snarl than a smile.

'Top hand?' Daybright ran an insolent gaze over Dallas's trail-worn clothes. 'To me, you look like a goddamn grubline rider, trying to sweet-talk me out of a free meal . . .' He flicked his gaze towards the tough cowboys, both solid, medium-sized men. 'Get rid of him.'

'Hey!' Dallas said as the men closed in and Daybright turned back towards his house. 'No need for any rough stuff! Who the hell you think you are?'

Daybright glanced over his shoulder. 'You're about to find out, drifter.' He chuckled and went on inside.

By then the first man, the one with the black hair and shadowed jawline even though Dallas could smell shaving-soap on him, gripped Marchant's arm and spun him around.

Dallas came easily, taking the man by surprise so that the cowboy hesitated in delivering the blow he had cocked and ready. Marchant stomped on his instep with his high-heeled riding-boot and as the man grunted and bent in the middle, he grabbed him by the shoulders and brought his knee up into his face.

The black-haired man spilled awkwardly to one side and the other man, red-haired, closed quickly, driving a blow into Dallas's kidney region. Marchant dropped to his knees, lights exploding behind his eyes, his entire body seared with pain, as Red came in swinging.

Dallas took a heavy blow to the back of the head, fell forward, but twisted half-way down and kicked the redhead's legs out from under him. As the man sprawled, the black-haired man staggered up, his face a mask of blood. He saw it glistening on his questing hand and roared a curse as he charged back in.

Dallas, still on his back, lifted up on to his shoulders and drove both boots into the man's groin. The black-haired man was out of it now but Red was still in and feeling mighty vicious. He came in with big fists swinging and Dallas caught two blows that staggered him. But he ducked under the third, belted Red's midriff with a blurring tattoo that made the man step back and sag in the middle.

Dallas whipped up his Peacemaker and slammed it across the man's head. Red dropped and the ranch door opened behind him. Dallas came round, gun in hand, but froze when he saw that Daybright was covering him with a cocked rifle.

'You're not the first drifter I've seen who can fight, mister, but you're the last one I want to see on my land . . . Now git. You've got ten seconds to climb into that saddle and ride out.'

Dallas went without comment, aching, his kidney region mighty sore. He had taken plenty of blows in that area when he had been in the Black Hell . . . maybe it would never have a chance to heal.

He quit Daybright's Top D under the curious and sometimes hostile gaze of the cowboys. He rode on into town, shadowed by two riders he was sure were on Daybright's payroll. *Making sure he cleared Top D land pronto.*

In town he had a few drinks, bought a few more for some locals, and by the time he turned into his bed in the room above the saloon bar, he thought about what he would do.

Now, riding down towards the Lindon spread, which bordered Top D's southern boundary, he knew what he was going to do.

CHAPTER 3

RESCUER

It was Jemma who became aware of the two riders first. Corey Lindon was busy with an auger, drilling holes for wooden pegs in the uprights and cross-beams of the fence he was building. He aimed to make it substantial as he had seen Top D cows roaming right over to this side of the creek and he knew once they saw Jemma's vegetable-patch they would use their weight to try and push down the fence.

Jemma, though absorbed in her gardening, caught a movement out of the corner of her eye and her heart beat faster as she thought it might be a deer. To her way of thinking, deer would be just as much a menace to her vegetable-patch as stray cattle. So, on her haunches, she turned quickly, using her trowel to steady herself. She frowned when she saw the two riders coming up from the creek.

They could only have come from Top D that way – and they had so far met no friendly riders from Daybright's spread.

'Corey! Corey!' When he glanced up, sawdust on his hands and some in his hair, she pointed with the trowel, standing herself now.

Lindon straightened hurriedly when he saw the riders, still clasping the T-shaped auger, his only weapon. He wiped an arm across his sweat-beaded forehead, a young face, free of crease-lines, just with a fair fluff of beard along the jawline. He was a man in his late twenties but looked younger.

'Howdy, gents,' he called, smiling. 'Do somethin' for you?'

The first man was solid-looking, but roughly dressed and that seemed to give him a threatening air even though he smiled back at Corey Lindon. He leaned his arms on his saddle horn, halting his mount by the ragged line of fencing.

'Yeah, reckon you can, Lindon.' He jerked his head at the portion of fence that had been erected and pre-drilled. But, as yet, Lindon hadn't made his pegs to drive home and lock everything in place. 'You gone an' built right across our cow trail to the crick.'

Lindon stiffened. '*Your* cow trail? But – if you're from Top D, then the cows would come down from the far side. My fence wouldn't hinder them.'

'Well, it sure ain't *gonna* hinder 'em, I can tell you that,' said the second man, shaggy-haired to the shoulders, looking at Jemma with beady eyes as she still stood rigidly in front of her garden patch. 'It's gotta come down. Mr Daybright said "Play it fair, men. Go warn him before he goes to all the trouble of buildin' that there fence." Sound fair enough?'

'No!' The word burst from Lindon and his hands tightened on the long auger. His heart was hammering and there was a faint trembly edge to his voice as he realized these men were here to make trouble, whatever they said. 'That – this fence is on our land and . . .'

The first man had shaken loose his lariat while Lindon's attention had been on his companion, and now he dropped a loop over the nearest uprights, supporting the cross-rails in their X-shaped angle.

'Corey!' cried Jemma and she turned to run for the cabin where they kept the shotgun.

But the shaggy-haired man laughed and rammed his horse between her and the cabin. She ran against the mount and he used its weight to knock her off her feet. As she sprawled she heard the splintering of the fence uprights as they cracked off at ground level, pulled by the other rider's rope.

Then the shaggy-haired man was in front of her, pulling her to her feet, laughing as she struck at his beefy shoulders with her trowel which he soon twisted from her fingers. He curled a muscled arm about her slim waist and pulled her against him, lowering his face towards hers.

Lindon stood poised but undecided. His fence was being demolished and his wife was being assaulted . . . With a wild yell he ran at the man pawing Jemma. Then there was a rifle shot and the man on the horse reeled as a bullet tore his hat from his head. A second shot clipped his left ear lobe and he spilled from the saddle, yelling '*Hey!*'

Lindon froze as did the shaggy-haired man and

even Jemma stopped struggling.

A tall, gaunt man came around the corner of the cabin, levering another shell into a smoking rifle. His face was hard and grim as he strode purposefully towards the shaggy man, who released the girl and stepped back, looking startled, one hand going out ahead of him as if he would push the stranger away.

'Now, wait a minute. . . !'

The rifle barrel smashed his hand aside and he howled. Then the butt slammed across his ribs. As he gagged, doubling up, the brass butt-plate cracked against his skull and stretched him out, moaning on the ground at Jemma Lindon's feet.

Dallas glanced at the frightened young woman.

'You all right, ma'am?'

She nodded, mouth too dry with recent fear to utter a word.

The black-haired man was on his feet now, holding his bleeding ear, watching warily as Dallas came towards him. He cringed a little under that bleak gaze, dropping his eyes to the menacing rifle barrel.

'Wait up! What the hell you doin'. . . ?'

'Stopping you from what *you*'re doing,' Dallas told him coldly.

'But. . . !'

'But nothing, feller. Get your pard and ride outta here pronto. Or the next bullet goes through both your feet.'

'Christ! We never . . .'

He broke off as the rifle barrel angled down and pointed towards his dusty boots. He scooped up his bullet-torn hat, jammed it on his head and helped the shaggy man to his feet and then into his saddle.

Minutes later they were going back across the creek towards the trail that led around the butte.

'Come from Top D, eh?' opined Dallas.

Lindon, a comforting arm around Jemma now, nodded.

'We – we're mighty obliged, Mr. . . ?'

'Dallas is close enough. You'd be the Lindons, I guess.'

Jemma, wiping her eyes, pushing some strands of hair back from her flushed face, glanced at him sharply.

'How did you know that?'

'Heard in town there was a couple of that name trying to prove-up along Comanche Creek. Wondered if you might need some help. With the homesteading, I mean.'

Lindon frowned.

'You mean – work for us?' He shook his head. 'Dallas, we're mighty glad for what you did, *al*mighty glad, and you're welcome to water your mount, have a meal, spend the night in that part of the barn that's finished, but – well, we don't have any money to hire anyone.'

Jemma frowned and tugged at his shirt. He looked down at her.

'No, Jemma, we don't! We have to think of the baby when it's due and . . .'

She's not long to go, Dallas thought, looking at the woman's waistline. *Just a few weeks, maybe . . .*

'Corey! This isn't the first time we've been rousted by Top D riders and it won't be the last. Neither of us

31

can hope to fight them. Daybright's a very powerful man and a rich one. He can hire some real hardcases – we wouldn't stand a chance!'

Dallas looked from one to the other.

'Folks, I have to tell you I've been in jail down in Mexico. I escaped and it's taken me best part of a year to get fit again. I need some steady work and – well, I once tried to prove-up on a quarter-section before I ran into the trouble that landed me in jail. I'm pretty good with hammer and saw and my old man taught me fencing while I was a shaver. I'd be willing to spend some time here just for grub and keep. . . .'

'We couldn't let you do that!' protested Lindon and there was pride in his voice that made Dallas smile a little in approval.

'Well, it's up to you.' Dallas didn't want to seem too damn eager. 'But this is good country. If you're having trouble with this Daybright – who I heard about in town, also – it wouldn't faze me any.'

Lindon snorted. 'You don't know him! I'd never seen those two before but I know he's got tougher men than them on his payroll.'

'Uh-huh – I'm used to tough men. But, as I say, folks, it's up to you. I'm not saying I'll stay permanent but I'll sure see you on your feet, and I'm your man if you have any trouble. . . .'

'You do a pretty good job of sellin' yourself,' Lindon said a trifle curtly but Dallas merely shrugged.

Jemma, still looking a bit uncertain, tugged at her husband's arm.

'Corey,' she said, 'let's go make a cup of coffee while Dallas tends to his horse and we can . . . talk about it inside, out of this wind.'

There was little wind down here but Dallas gave no sign that he knew she was just making an excuse to speak to her husband in private.

He touched a hand to his hatbrim, walked back around the cabin and brought his grey into the yard, taking it across to the well. He pumped some water into the trough and while the animal drank, splashed water over his face and neck.

Then they called him to the cabin and he went in, hat in hands. It was sparsely furnished but neat and the woman had bleached some floursacks, hemmed them with coloured thread and picked out a few butterfly designs in various shapes, using them as table-covers and half-curtains.

Coffee and warmed-over biscuits were on the table and before he had finished his first cup of java, Lindon cleared his throat and told him they would be proud to have him stay with them for as long as he liked. He didn't seem all that happy about it, mind.

'If we start to make a little money,' he added, 'after we round up some mavericks in the hills, then we'll see about payin' you somethin'.'

Dallas smiled.

'Fair enough. I have to go into town to settle a couple of things, but I ought to be back by sundown. I don't reckon those hardcases'll show up again, but you work with your shotgun handy to be on the safe side.'

Corey Lindon didn't like Dallas giving him orders

but he nodded curtly and Jemma, smiling, handed Dallas a small package in greasy paper.

'A little cold venison to see you to town and back.'

Dallas thanked her and rode out.

'I sure hope we're doin' the right thing,' Corey Lindon said.

'Look at it this way, Corey. Can we afford *not* to take his offer. . . ?'

He frowned. 'Ye-ah . . . but . . . well, he looks a hard man, Jem. I've got a strange feelin' about the way he turned up here. And those men: I've never seen them on Top D and most of Daybright's riders have been by to just look us over. . . .'

She blinked, started to say something, but changed her mind. A couple of creases appeared between her eyes.

The two hardcases were waiting for him on the town side of the pass. It was early afternoon when Dallas rode unsuspectingly through the narrow pass. Then they came out of the shadows, on their mounts, rifles in hands.

He reined up the grey and sat his saddle in the middle of the trail, careful to keep his hands in full sight.

'Thought we were going to meet back of the saloon, gents,' he said quietly.

The black-haired one touched his raw, blood-caked ear. 'This wasn't part of the deal!' he snapped.

The shaggy-haired one's hat sat lopsided on his swollen head and he touched it with one hand.

'Nor was this. The hell you think you were doin'?

You said you'd just put a gun on us and run us off!'

'There was nothing about wrecking his fence – or attacking the woman.' Dallas's lips seemed hardly to move as he spoke, something he had learned in the Black Hell where talking between prisoners was banned. He flicked his cold eyes from one to the other. 'Lucky I arrived when I did.'

Although he was holding a gun, the black-haired man felt uneasy under that bleak stare.

'Hell. Made it look better, din' it? Bit of rough stuff, then you comin' in and chasin' us off. . . .'

The shaggy-haired one licked his lips.

'Me and Jed want more money,' he said.

Dallas smiled thinly.

'There ain't no more. I told you what I'd pay you for turning up at the Lindons and threatening them in Daybright's name. You've got half – I'm here to pay you the rest.'

'We want more!' snapped Jed, then swallowed when Dallas's eyes swung to him. 'Just like Morg said – we din' figure on gettin' shot at or havin' our heads busted.'

'Told you – there's no more. I'll pay you what we agreed on, but there's no more.'

'Yeah? Well, maybe we'll just see about that!' Morg's voice was rough but shaky. Still he was determined on this. 'We could ride back to Lindon's and tell 'em the whole story.'

'If you've a hankering to be buried out there by that pretty little creek, you could.'

Jed frowned. 'Listen, we don't know you. Never seen you before you approached us in that saloon bar. You look tough but right now, you're the one under *our* guns. You better think about that.'

'I am.'

Suddenly the Peacemaker was blazing in Dallas's right hand. Jed yelled wildly as he threw up his arms and somersaulted over his mount's rump. Morg's shaggy hair flew wild about his shoulders as he plunged to one side and rolled on the ground, clasping at his bleeding upper right arm.

Jed got to his feet groggily, shaking his head, a fresh red scar across his left cheek, blood dripping from his jaw.

Dallas sat his saddle casually, even smiling faintly as he covered them with the smoking gun and fumbled in his jacket pocket with his left hand. He tossed a small drawstring poke on the ground between the two scared hardcases. Coins clinked as dust rose around it.

'Your money, gents. Now I don't want to see either of you again. Go on back to town.'

He rode at their skittish mounts, loosed two shots into the air. The horses snorted and whickered as they ran off down the trail.

'Hey! Jesus! It's four mile back to town!' protested Jed, holding a filthy kerchief against his bleeding face.

'Hurry it up some and you'll make it by sundown. *Adios*, boys. There better not be any *hasta la vistas*.'

Dallas spun his grey and rode back through the pass. He stopped on the other side and reloaded his pistol, pleased with the way he had gotten the gun out so fast and working. Mind, his shots had been a little off, but he figured those two had learned their lessons.

He rode on again at a slow pace, aiming to make the Lindon place around sundown, just as if he had ridden all the way into town and back.

CHAPTER 4

THE WHIP

Tag Daybright looked across his cluttered desk at the man everyone called 'the Whip'. He was Aaron Whipple, ramrod of the Top D, lanky with thick wrists and hands like post-hole shovels. His features were heavy, but not gross, and there was a blankness about his pale eyes that even Daybright found unsettling at times.

Whipple was a man about thirty, with string-coloured hair and addicted to chain-smoking. If he wasn't rolling a cigarette he was smoking one – or a cigarillo, cheroot, cigar. He had even been known to chew tobacco. He was addicted to nicotine but no one in his right mind would tell him so. Most men, with even basic wisdom, sensed the power and dislike for human beings in general in the man and gave him a wide berth.

'What is it, Whip?' Daybright asked now as

Whipple exhaled smoke, coughing some before speaking.

'Tommy Snell.'

Daybright arched his eyebrows. 'He's s'posed to have gone into town to pick up those legal papers from Cash Bridges.'

Whipple nodded. 'That he did.' He produced two thick manila envelopes tied with pink string and placed them on the desk. The rancher still looked curious. 'Stopped off for a drink in the saloon, which is OK, I guess. But he said Jed Handley and Ray Morgan were drinkin'. Looked like they'd been on it all night – and still had money.'

Daybright was interested now, set aside the legal papers he had been inspecting.

'What'd those two been doin' to earn any money?'

'That's it, Tag. Jed's got the lobe of his left ear missin'. Morg's head's all lopsided. They claim they were roustin' the Lindons and some drifter showed up, jumped the pair of 'em.'

Daybright's hands clenched and the pencil he was holding snapped. 'Drifter? Who. . . ?'

Whipple shrugged. 'Sounded a little like that feller you threw off and who beat up on Curly and Sandy. But thing is, Morg let slip they'd said we sent 'em to roust them homesteaders.'

'They *what*!' Daybright was standing now, anger darkening his face. 'By hell, the day I have to hire deadbeats like them two. . . ! Why would they say that?'

'I dunno. But figured you might like me to ride into town and find out.'

Daybright took a turn around the desk, stopped by a window and looked through the dusty pane at men working in the ranch yard.

'You do that. Find out about this drifter too. If it's the same one was lookin' for work out here – well, I wonder if Lindon give him a job?'

'I'll ride on by the spread on the way to town. You want me to run Morgan and Handley outta town?'

'See what they got to say for themselves. You decide.'

Whipple nodded, opened the door, flicked away his cigarette butt and, as he walked across the ranch yard, calling to the wrangler to saddle his horse, he took out tobacco sack and papers and began building another smoke.

Tag Daybright watched him, frowning.

He'd had a bad feeling about that drifter.

A *bad* feeling.

Dallas was splitting lodgepole pine for fence-post uprights. He paused, examined the axe blade, then walked across to the grindstone in its weathered frame and pumped the treadle, running the blade across the stone, sparks fanning into the sunlight.

Corey Lindon was cutting wooden pegs down by the incomplete barn and Jemma was cooking something in the house. Smelt like bread and Dallas thought back to when he and Carrie had first set up their cabin on their quarter-section. That smell took him back to those days. . . .

He lifted his gaze across the creek, followed it down to where it swung out of sight and beyond that to where Lindon had already marked out the line between his land and that of Tag Daybright.

Right across there, he thought, looking at the undulating land. *That's where it had been, where they had pinned all their hopes. Now what was left of the cabin was no more than a heap of rotting logs and caved-in sod roof.*

He paused in sharpening the axe, straightened a little, scanning the land over there, now part of Top D.

The grave should be round about where that small rise was. Long obliterated, probably. . . .

'I've about finished the pegs.'

Dallas turned slowly at the sound of Lindon's voice, saw the man standing with a lot of short rounded pegs held in a folded gunnysack. Lindon looked proud of himself.

'Didn't take me as long as I thought.'

'You have to strip the bark off first, else it'll rot, dry out and then the pegs will be loose in the holes.'

Lindon flushed.

'Yeah – forgot. Carried away with cuttin' 'em up the right length. Guess I'm pretty much of a greenhorn.'

'We all got to learn. Should be ready to start putting in the uprights after lunch.'

'All right.' Lindon sounded a little hesitant or distracted and Dallas turned to look in the direction the man was staring.

Over by the creek, watering his horse, was a tall rider, rolling a cigarette, a heel hooked over his saddle horn, watching them.

'One of Daybright's crew?' asked Dallas.

'His ramrod – Aaron Whipple. They call him "the Whip". He claims it's because he's whipped every man he's ever fought.'

'You sound worried.'

'Well, what's he doin'? Why's he watchin' us?'

'Sticky-beaking. Watching your progress. Daybright roust you much?'

'No-o. Not too much, strangely enough.' Then Lindon's mouth tightened and he added quietly, 'He once told me to go ahead and prove-up – if I could. That right now we didn't bother him. That when we did, he'd just move in and take over.' He lifted a haunted gaze to Dallas's face. 'It was the way he said it. Contemptuous. As if we didn't matter a damn to him. Just a couple of insects to be swatted aside when he felt like it.'

Dallas kept watching Whipple as the man lit his smoke.

'Daybright's got plenty of land now. He likely won't bother you.'

Lindon snorted. 'He's not worried about our land. He just doesn't want neighbours; likes his solitude, he says. "Once you got a couple snotty-nosed kids runnin' around, that might bother me," he told us. Like he was puttin' a time-limit on us.'

Dallas nodded. *Arrogant. Power complex,* he allowed silently.

Just the kind of son of a bitch he hated most. He had learned in prison that hate was pretty much a futile thing. But now and again he came across someone he could take the time to vent his frustrations on.

42

Looked like he had a target now: a bonus added to what he already had planned.

Jed and Morg didn't stand a chance.

The Whip was waiting for them behind the saloon when they made one of their trips to the privy. He let them relieve themselves, then, when they came back, he stepped out behind them, placed a big hand on Morg's swollen head, his other on Jed's wounded ear.

They had little time to feel pain before he slammed their heads together. They moaned, staggering. But Whipple held them, crunched their skulls together again, them slammed them back against the clapboard wall. Their legs gave way and they sat down, moaning.

The Whip stood above them, hands on hips, burning cigarette between his heavy lips. He kicked Morgan on the shin and the man howled, snatched at his throbbing leg. Jed started to curl his legs up out of the way but Whipple's boot drove hard into his ribs and the man gagged, rolled on to his side in the dirt, writhing.

Whipple leaned down, blowing tobacco smoke into their contorted faces.

'Gents, you are outta your class. The hell you think you were doin', tellin' that sodbuster Lindon Tag'd sent you to roust him?'

They both stopped their groaning and looked up with pained eyes, glancing at each other worriedly.

Whip drew back one of his big boots and they cringed, trying to press back into the clapboards.

'Don't!' piped Morg.

'I'm waitin'. You got about half a second. . . .'

They both started talking together and Whip sighed, backhanded the luckless Morgan across his already swollen head. The man clutched at his face and rolled away, almost crying. Jed ran a tongue around his lips.

'Feller – paid us – forty bucks.'

Whip arched his heavy eyebrows.

'To roust the Lindons?'

Jed nodded quickly.

'Yeah. To say Daybright sent us. Then he appeared and kicked us off. Wanted to get in good with that greenhorn, I guess.'

Whipple pursed his lips, burning cigarette hanging from his bottom lip. 'Get in good enough so he could go work for 'em. Now, I doubt any man is that hard up for a job he has to rig things that-a-way.'

'I – dunno. Just what I told you. He paid us, then shot us up a little. Just scrapes but – well, man, he's fast with that Peacemaker and ain't afraid to use it.'

'Uh-huh. This drifter interests me. Sounds like a hardcase. Asked for work at Top D, boss said "no". Hires you two to fake a roust so's he can step in and play hero. Just so he could go work for a greenhorn sodbuster. Now, I wonder what in hell is behind that. . . ?'

It bothered Whipple. He simply couldn't figure it. Nor could Tag Daybright, but the rancher was a mite worried. He had seen Dallas in action, knew the man was tough – sure not the type to help out a struggling greenhorn like Corey Lindon. . . .

'Keep a watch on that hardcase, Whip. Sooner or

later he's gonna go to town. You have a talk with him when he does.'

Whipple smiled thinly as he rolled his cigarette paper around the tobacco, licked it and stuck it in a corner of his mouth.

'Pleasure, Tag. Pure . . . pleasure.'

Corey Lindon was a mite ashamed of himself.

He was sending Dallas into town with the buckboard to pick up some things at the general store. Normally he would go himself, maybe with Jemma for company, but he always had to run the gauntlet of rough taunting by some of the cowboys lounging around the boardwalks and twice he had come close to getting into a fight.

Jemma had kept him out of it but it only made the taunts worse.

'What's it like hidin' behind them skirts, greenhorn?'

'I wouldn't mind getting that close to them skirts, come to think of it.'

'Hey, sodbuster. Ain't it hard on the knees, hunkerin' down like that behind a woman. . . ?'

It bothered Lindon. He knew he wasn't much of a fighter and he was kind of scared by the prospect of ever having forcibly to defend himself – or, worse, Jemma – with his fists, but he felt kind of craven after those roustings.

So, when they needed more nails and some rope and wire, and Jemma found she was short of flour and raisins and some other things, Corey asked Dallas would he run the errand.

Dallas looked him over, saw the worry with the

45

touch of shame and nodded.

'Yeah. Got a thing or two I'd like to do in town, so I'll do the chore.'

Lindon was grateful and his hand shook a little as he counted out some money from his meagre supply.

'Could you bring somethin' – nice – back for Jemma?' he asked quietly.

'Nice?'

'Yeah – well, you know . . .'

'No. I don't.'

'Stuff a woman might like. Ribbon for her bonnet. Piece of fancy soap. . . .'

Dallas hesitated – he couldn't see himself asking for anything like that. But in the end he agreed. He hitched up the team and rode out early one morning.

Jemma and Lindon waved him off.

'I wouldn't have minded a trip to town,' the woman said and Corey forced a smile.

'Thought you and me might make time for one a little later. Just us two.'

He slid an arm about her waist and she smiled as she leaned her head against his shoulder.

'That would be nice, Corey. Real nice.'

Dallas enjoyed the morning. It was bright and sunny and crisp, but not cold enough to keep his jacket buttoned. He liked this country, kind of regretted that his original plan to prove-up on land here with Carrie hadn't worked out.

He would never get a second chance like that – but then, these days, he wasn't looking for one.

46

When he had what he wanted, he would likely end up a long way from here – a *long* way.

He flicked the reins at the team and the buckboard clattered along the trail to town.

He was loading the buckboard at the small dock outside Shackleton's general store, struggling with the hundred-pound keg of nails, when he heard the footfall on the planks beside him.

Dallas looked up at the tall, gangly man silhouetted against the bright sun. He couldn't make out features but he knew by the man's general build that he was the rider he had seen down at Comanche Creek, watching the Lindon place.

'Lend you a hand,' Whipple said, jumping down beside him, jamming his cigarette between his lips. Together they lifted the heavy keg. The buckboard springs sagged and squeaked as they manoeuvred it into position in the middle of the tray.

'Thanks.'

Whip waved it away, stepped back and dusted off his hands as he looked over the goods already stacked there: bags of flour, parcels of various items, a smaller keg of tenpenny nails, the larger keg, some coils of plain wire. He picked up a ragged leaflet that was caught under one of these coils and his heavy features straightened out as he read. He set his hard eyes on Dallas.

'*Glidden's Barbed Wire.* Figurin' on usin' some?'

Dallas took the leaflet, folded it and stuffed it into his shirt pocket.

'Shackleton tried to sell me some. I'll let Lindon decide.'

47

'Uh-huh. Wouldn't recommend it myself. Tears up the cattle.'

'That's the idea. They nudge it once, they usually got enough brains not to do it again.'

'Had experience with this stuff?'

Dallas shook his head.

'I've been away. This has only just hit the market according to Shackleton. Been other barbed wire but this one seems to be the best. Cheap, got the barbs woven in between the strands.'

'Lindon might find himself in a heap of trouble he starts usin' it.'

Dallas shrugged.

'I think he's expecting trouble anyway. From Daybright.'

'Well, what you expect? Homesteadin' land right next to the biggest cattle spread in the county.'

'Biggest?'

'Will be.'

Dallas grunted, locked up the tailgate.

'Thanks for the help, Whip.'

'You know me?'

'Heard a little.'

'Got an advantage then. I ain't heard a thing about you. 'Cept you're nursemaidin' that greenhorn sodbuster. Makes a man wonder why.'

'Keep on wondering.' Dallas started towards the driving seat but Whipple grabbed his arm with a big hand.

'S'pose you tell me – now!'

He shoved Dallas roughly against the buckboard, hard enough to make it sway on its springing.

He breathed smoke from his dangling cigarette into Dallas's face.

'*Right* now!'

CHAPTER 5

'WHIP' WHIPPED

Dallas felt a bolt head on the buckboard grinding against his spine as Whipple leaned his weight on him, using his elbows now to rake his ribs.

Whipple grinned around his cigarette, sure of himself.

Until Dallas's knee lifted towards his crotch. Then he jumped back hurriedly, turning with years of fighting experience and taking the blow on the outside of his thigh. Even so, the force of it sent him staggering and Dallas jerked free, spun back. His fist took Whip on the side of the jaw, snapping the man's head around so that he stumbled face first into the rough wood of the buckboard's side. Splinters tore at his flesh and he grunted, grabbing at the vehicle for support.

He held on with one hand, swung wide, his other arm arcing around, the fist taking Dallas across the side of the head. The drifter staggered and Whipple thrust away from the buckboard.

By now, men on the boardwalks had stopped to watch. Someone yelled 'Fight! Fight!' and brought a dozen more running down Main, dust spurting from beneath their anxious boots.

Whip circled Dallas quickly as the man staggered, watching for his opening, fists cocked in front of his face. He jabbed with a right, knocked Dallas's hat off. But the drifter had ducked, too, came up inside the next blow and ripped four savage blows into the man's midriff. Whipple wasn't used to taking punishment, only to dishing it out. Hard knuckles driving into his mid-section, making his ribs creak, were almost forgotten sensations, it had been so long since anything like that had happened to him.

But the shortness of breath and searing pain the punches brought with them, made Whipple stop dead. He pushed Dallas's next blow aside, stepped right – smack into the path of the drifter's left. His head snapped back on his shoulders and he stumbled, shock as much as pain reeling him off balance.

Dallas stepped closer, hammered aside Whip's defence and hooked the man under the jaw. Whipple's eyes crossed and he grasped at the buckboard's tailgate for support, struck his head on the edge of the hardwood board. Skin burst and blood flowed – and that was what brought a roar of realization to Whip's throat: he was *taking* punishment and doing nothing about it!

He stepped forward with one long stride to meet Dallas's forward motion and their hard bodies met with a jolt. They both stepped back, instantly lunged forward again.

There was a vicious flurry of fists, driving midriff blows, wild swings, straight jabs that snapped both men's heads on their shoulders. Blood sprayed and skin tore. The crowd roared – they had never seen Whipple back-pedalling before, face streaked with blood, shirt torn, shaking his head jerkily as he tried to clear his vision. Dallas stalked him and the crowd swayed, giving them room. Whipple's heel caught on the edge of the boardwalk and he sprawled. Dallas went after him but the man spun to hands and knees, leapt on to the loading platform, swung a boot at head-height.

It slammed alongside Dallas's right ear. He stumbled and staggered, eventually going down, half-way across the street. Whipple bared his teeth and leapt at his flailing form, both boots thrust out before him.

Dallas glimpsed those spurs and the high heels, rolled away. Whip jarred to the ground, close enough for one spur to rake down Dallas's back, ripping open his shirt. Dallas grunted at the sear of pain as the rowel sliced his flesh, spun away and drove both his own boots at the big ramrod as he lunged back.

They took Whip in the chest and he grunted, slid off, putting down one hand to steady himself. Dallas kicked the arm out from under him and Whipple slammed to the dust. Dallas kicked him a glancing blow in the head, somersaulted backwards, staggering some as he lunged to his feet. Whip had been slowed down but he came up with a handful of dirt and Dallas spread a hand in front of his face as gravel stung him. He blinked, momentarily blinded, and the ramrod charged in, head down, arms wide and grappling. He caught Dallas by the hips and rammed his head into the man's midriff like a buffalo protecting its young. Dallas's legs quivered. He grabbed wildly at the bent shoulders as Whipple pulled back and drove his head in again.

Dallas twisted, took some of the blow on his ribs – and they creaked audibly – then twisted Whip's ears, bringing a howl of pain that echoed down the far-from-silent street. Still holding the man's blood-slippery ears, Dallas heaved Whipple forward, swiftly changed his grip, one hand in the man's hair, the other on his belt.

With a grunting roar of effort he ran the doubled-over ramrod at the buckboard and rammed his head between the spokes of the large rear wheel. The team snorted and danced and the vehicle moved a little, a spoke jamming against Whip's neck. He gagged and choked, tongue protruding. Dallas limped behind him, took deliberate aim, and hammered a fist down on to the man's kidneys.

Whipple's legs collapsed and his neck jammed tighter. Someone started yelling that Whip was going to have his neck broke. . . . Another two men grabbed at the rearing team, gentling them, calming them so that the buckboard moved only a few inches back and forth.

It took three men to get Whipple free and he was unconscious when they dropped him on the ground, his neck raw and bruised. Dallas merely stared down at him, boots spread, wiping his face with his shirtsleeve.

He turned as a hand touched his shoulder. He saw

a shortish middle-aged man with a tin star pinned to his shirt.

'Step back, mister! I'm Sheriff Garner.'

Dallas glanced at him and started to step around him, towards the boardwalk and the entrance to the store.

'Where the hell you think you're goin'?' demanded the sheriff, a hand on the butt of his six-gun now.

Dallas spat some blood and felt a tooth that seemed loose in his gums before answering.

'Forgot some soap.'

The crowd went into stunned silence. Garner frowned, looked puzzledly at the crowd, and then turned back to Dallas. He grinned sourly, pulled a face.

'Soap . . .' The word was flat, yet querying.

'Yeah – something – scented.'

Someone snickered and Garner scowled.

'*Scented* soap! For Chris'sakes!'

'I like to smell – nice,' Dallas said, deadpan, and stumbled towards the door of the store. The grinning crowd made way for him, a couple even bowing, sweeping off their hats.

Garner stood there beside the bloody, uncon-scious form of Whip Whipple, scratching his head, hat half-raised.

'Well, we get all kinds,' he sighed, following Dallas.

As soon as Corey Lindon saw Dallas drive into the yard, he noticed the state of the man's face, dropped his tools and came hurrying across.

'My God! What happened?'

His exclamation brought Jemma to the door and she also registered shock. She came to where Dallas had stopped the buckboard and was already lowering the tailgate. He moved stiffly.

'Met Whipple.'

'He – attacked you?' asked the girl.

'Yes, ma'am. We had a little go-round.'

'Have you seen a doctor?'

Dallas shook his head, started to drag some of the goods on to the lowered tailgate, ready to unload.

'I've had worse than this.'

'My God – where?' Jemma was aghast as she saw the bruises and cuts and swellings.

Dallas shrugged, glanced at Corey.

'Want to lend a hand with this here keg?'

As they lowered it to the ground, Lindon asked hesitantly:

'Did you – beat Whip?'

'Well, he was lying unconscious in the street when I left. Sheriff wasn't too happy but the crowd seemed to have enjoyed the fight.'

'I'll bet!' Lindon was staring at Dallas, mouth a little slack. 'There've been so many stories about Whipple. He's never been beaten in a fight.'

'Has now.'

Jemma and her husband exchanged a glance; it was a mixture of puzzlement and pleasure. Then Lindon sobered.

'Tag Daybright must've set him on you, Dallas. He won't like this.'

'My worry – and it don't worry me none at all.'

'You wouldn't say that if you knew more about Daybright,' Jemma told him. 'He can be mighty mean if he doesn't get his own way.'

'Well, I don't aim to bring trouble on you folks, but I'm here to tell you that Tag Daybright and me are gonna lock horns if he keeps after me.'

Both the Lindons looked worried as Dallas unloaded the rest of the goods and handed Corey the ragged leaflet on Gliddens barbed wire.

'Might be worth thinking about. . . .'

Lindon paled as he read.

'I – I had thought about it. But – truth is, Dallas, I'm not – game to try it. There's the expense, too, of course, but if I string barbed wire, Daybright will ride roughshod over us and drive us off our land.'

'You're on prove-up. Call in the law. He can't buck that.'

Jemma smiled bitterly.

'They say Otis Garner is Daybright's man when it suits him. Now come on into the house while I see what I can do for some of those cuts.'

Tag Daybright couldn't stop looking at Whipple. Never before had he seen the man marked-up in any way. But now the heavy features were all distorted with swellings and cuts and spreading bruises. The man moved as if he had aged twenty years since he rode into town. He nursed the whiskey Tag had poured for him, almost afraid to drink. The liquor bit savagely into the deep cuts on his mouth.

'Man's hard as a goddamn tree,' he said quietly, his voice hoarse, purpling ridges running up from his neck and along his swollen jaw. 'I put him down several times but he just kept bouncin' back.'

Daybright continued to stare, rolling his own drink glass around in his fingers, apparently unaware of it.

'If Dallas hadn't come here first lookin' for work, I'd begin to think Lindon had sent for him – wanted a hardcase on his payroll.'

Whip snorted and immediately regretted it: his nose was swollen and tender, hammered to one side.

'Well, Lindon's a 'fraidy cat. He needs backin'.'

Tag scowled.

'Yeah. It's why I never bothered with him much. He's a greenhorn, feelin' his way, soft Easterner, dunno how to fight for his rights. Figured I'd just leave him sit till I was good and ready to kick him off that land.'

'Might dig in his heels now he's got Dallas.'

'Yeah.' Daybright's frown deepened. 'Wonder why Dallas went to Lindon after lookin' for work here with cattle. Homesteadin's a heap different to ranch work.'

Whip shrugged and even that hurt. His only interest in Dallas now was when and how he was going to get a chance to square things.

'Maybe he just liked this neck of the woods,' he said casually and risked a sip at the whiskey, swearing as it bit into his lips.

Tag Daybright snapped up his head.

'Now, I wonder . . . He comes here out of the blue, asks for a job, says someone told him in town that I was hirin' – which is eyewash. If I want to hire someone I know where to send for the kind of men I want ridin' for me. We throw him off – kinda – and next thing he's workin' for our closest neighbour, doin' homestead chores. A man who can beat up two of my men, whip the daylights outta you and, accordin' to Morg and Jed, can use a gun faster'n anyone they've ever seen. Now, you tell me what a man like that is doin' workin' for a greenhorn sodbuster – right next door to me.'

Whip blinked: his head was throbbing and he wasn't thinking very fast.

'You know him from somewhere?'

Daybright shook his head.

'Pretty sure I don't. Go tell Garner to find out what he can about him. See if there's any dodgers out on him. Man like that can't just appear without someone knowin' somethin' about him.'

Whip moaned.

'I gotta ride all the way back to town? Can't you send someone in to Garner?'

Tag's eyes narrowed.

'I'm sendin' you. You're the one didn't do your chore properly. Now you go put it right.'

'I should've been with him.'

Jemma, cutting up vegetables, glanced up sharply at her husband. She could see Dallas through the doorway, walking across the yard to unhitch the buckboard. She had washed and bathed his wounds, dabbed on iodine, but the man hadn't seemed unduly bothered by any pain.

'What good would that have done, Corey?'

58

He looked at her, eyes haunted. 'Because – I – I think I'm a coward, Jem.'

'No!' She set down the knife and came swiftly around the table to stand by his chair, slipping an arm about his shoulders. 'That's not true, Corey! It's just that this is so – different, this life we're leading now. Nothing in your past has prepared you for this kind of – pioneer work. I think you've done wonders since we took up this land. If we just mind our business and work hard to prove-up, we'll make a niche for ourselves in the community and – you'll feel better then when we have friends we can go calling on or invite over. . . .'

He smiled and covered one of her small hands with his own – calloused now, losing its softness after months of work on the land.

'You're good support, Jem. But I've had a pretty soft life. You're right in that I wasn't prepared for this. But it's somethin' I've always wanted to do . . . be independent, build my own house for my wife and family.' He let the words trail off and added quietly, 'I have somethin' to prove to both our families back in Virginia. Neither really approved of our marriage.'

Which was why we ran away and had some strange preacher read us the vows, thought the girl but aloud she said:

'We're doing fine, Corey. You've worked hard. I – kind of like it here and at least I'd had cooking lessons at school which came in handy!' She laughed a little and he smiled, nodding. 'We'll prove-up. Now you stop worrying about your courage. It took plenty of that to pull up our roots and come all the way out here to start a fresh life.'

'I s'pose you're right, Jem.' But he couldn't shake the thought that deep down he was yellow.

He wasn't a man used to violence, not even used to hostility from unexpected quarters, and he was confused. When you got right down to it, he simply didn't know *how* to react.

He glanced out the door and saw Dallas leading the buckboard team back to the corrals.

Maybe *he* was the answer. Dallas had more or less forced himself upon them and he had sensed right off that there was a power and a strength in this stranger that he could draw on. Dallas had already proved he was willing to fight on the Lindons' behalf, seemed totally unafraid.

Yes, Corey Lindon decided, he could learn much from Dallas. And he would *have* to if he was going to survive. . . .

Tag Daybright was more worried about this Dallas than he was letting show.

A man who had always had something to hide, some deal going that chipped away at the edge of the law, he was suspicious of anything he didn't organize himself or was able to take control of easily.

This Dallas wasn't going to be anyone he could control. Not without a lot of trouble – and he could do without that right now. Before him were spread the legal papers Tommy Snell had brought out from Lawyer Bridges. They detailed all the land that had been available for proving-up, most of which he had managed to 'acquire' one way or another since he had moved in to the high plains. His aim was to make all the plains his, part of Top D, biggest ranch in the county, a power to be reckoned with in the cattle business.

He had to *appear* strictly legitimate or Bridges would never be able to swing these deals that allowed him to move in on homesteaders doing their best to prove-up. Sure he used his men to harass them but in such a way that if there was any real legal issue, he could point to one or two of his troublemakers, claim they acted off their own bat, and then fire them. Later, he would set them up on quarter-sections adjacent to his land, give them backing, and buy the land when they had proved-up. All legal – and all additions to the growing size of Top D.

He tried to concentrate on his forward planning now, but Dallas kept creeping into his thoughts and, angrily, he dragged the original county map which had been surveyed ten years ago towards him, looking at the land he had drawn into his ownership, ticking it off against a list Bridges had sent, detailing position, boundaries and area.

Suddenly he froze.

Names had been written in by the Land Agency, the names of the original homesteaders. Some had proved-up, some had failed. These latter had had a red-ink line drawn through their names.

He had been studying the creek land worked now by the Lindons, trying to figure out the best place to throw a dam up across Comanche Creek. There had been one flash flood last year and he aimed to stop it happening again by means of a dam to control the flow – even if it meant starving a bunch of nesters downstream for water. He could do it 'legally', he knew, if he paid money into the right hands. . . .

A name caught his attention, on a quarter-section he had long ago acquired, adjacent to the Lindons' place and now part of Top D. This was the land that had been scoured by the flood, prime grazing, all but ruined and only now starting to regenerate.

But eight years ago it had been worked by homesteaders. They had failed, apparently, and there was a red line drawn through their names, his own inked in above as subsequent legal purchaser and owner.

The original homesteaders' names beneath his were *D. and C. Marchant*

CHAPTER 6

THE OLD RANGER

Sheriff Otis Garner sat back solidly in his chair and squinted up at the battered Whipple. He would have liked to have made a joking remark about the man's injuries but Whipple wasn't a man to joke with over such things. Or anything else. Garner cleared his throat, frowning.

'I don't have time to be sendin' all over the goddamn country for old Wanted dodgers, Whip. Jesus, I've got enough on my plate as it is.'

'Tag wants it done.' Flatly. An order.

Garner sighed.

'Look, Shackleton's got in some of that new barbed wire. It's cheaper than any before. He's already got orders from Hanrahan and Flute and Callum. Other homesteaders are just waitin' on the sidelines to see what happens when they string it. You know what's gonna happen. Most of 'em are Top D's neighbours and Tag's gonna go through the roof

63

and I'll be up to my ass in work tryin' to keep the peace. He'll shoot 'em all if I don't step in. . . .'

Whip leaned his big hands on the edge of the desk and looked down at the lawman.

'Tag – wants – it –done. Now you do it, Otis, or I'll come round and rip that star off your shirt and shove it up your ass.'

Garner slumped.

'OK, OK. But what's so important about this Dallas? We all know he can fight and that he's Lindon's man, but why don't Tag just run him off like he did plenty of others? I'll look the other way.'

'You wanna ask him, go ahead. But I wouldn't, not till I'd found out if there're any Wanted dodgers on the son of a bitch, if I was you.'

'Well. Leave it with me. I dunno who's gonna pay for all the damn telegrams. . . .' He glanced up hopefully but Whip's battered face was dead sober.

'You get answers quick as you can. Start by lookin' through your own drawers. You must have a heap of old dodgers in there. You ain't the first sheriff here, you know.'

Whipple was right. There were plenty of old dodgers stacked up in the bottom of the cupboard and after the big foreman had left, Garner squatted down and pulled them out. He began sorting through them desultorily, stubborn, reluctant, but knowing that in the end he was going to have to send all those wires.

Trouble was, he'd only been sheriff here for five or six years. There had been one man before him, Anderson, but he had had to quit because of his wife's health. Then there had been a dead space for most of a year before Garner had gotten the job.

He didn't find any dodgers on Dallas Marchat but something stirred in the back of his mind. There had been some sort of enquiry about a . . . Marchant? Markwell? No! Markham! That was it! Though the other two names were mentioned.

'A Ranger!' he said aloud, snapping his fingers now. 'What the hell was his name. . . ? Walked with a limp . . . Lots of grey in his stubble. Sour as all hell, said he was gonna have to retire because of his hip wound and he wanted to track down the son of a bitch who had given it to him before he turned in his badge.'

He thought some more, packed a pipe and got it going, nodding as smoke curled up around his face. *Parry! That was the name! Yeah, it was coming back to him now. . . .*

Parry was a big man, never smiled, took himself and his job seriously. When he sat down, he shoved his right leg out straight before him, rubbed absently at his aching hip as he spoke.

'Only thing I'm sure about is he's a Texan. Sometimes calls himself "Dallas" and tags on "Markham" or "Markwell" or maybe "Marchant". Some name like that. Other times he's just "Texas".'

'What's he done?'

Parry snorted, his drooping moustache seeming to rear up from his seamed lower face with the sound.

'Rode with a wild bunch, their stampin' ground anywhere between Utah and Colorado and New

65

Mexico into north Texas. Once, we think, they hit a riverboat in Louisiana.'

'Robbers?'

'You bet. Banks, stages, once an army pay-train, mine pay-rolls, and railroad express cars.'

'Judas priest! I've never heard of 'em.'

'Right after the War. They kept on the move. Many a time I went clear outta my jurisdiction, over state lines, followin' leads.'

'Never caught 'em?'

'Oh, yeah. We caught up with 'em eventually. At Amarillo. Cornered 'em in a bank hold-up we'd set up. Big shoot-out.' Bitterly, he slapped his right hip. 'I had this feller "Texas" trapped in an old adobe shack. I'd been countin' bullets, was separated from the rest of my troop, and went in when I figured he was outta ammo.' He bared tobacco-stained teeth and shook his head. 'He had one bullet left – and he put it into my hip. My *God* it hurt! Busted up the bone like broken china, set me a'screamin' and writhin'. Son of a bitch took all my guns, all my money, all my bullets. Stopped long enough to wrap an old shirt round the wound, then rode out. Took my goddamn mount, too.' Parry paused, thinking about that terrible day, and his mouth tightened. 'Last time I seen him—'

'How long ago?'

'Be three years now.'

'And you're still after him?'

Bleak eyes sought Garner's.

'Only case I never closed in my en-tire career. I want to tie it up before I have to quit. Can't hardly sit

66

a saddle for more'n a couple hours at a time these days.'

Garner shook his head.

'Can't help you, Parry. I ain't been here long but I've never heard of this feller.'

'No. Was just a wild hope. Truth is, I ain't even sure this "Dallas" is the same man goin' by the monicker of "Texas", but I'm desperate. I'm the only one who's seen his face. They were masked in every job they pulled but he had nothin' coverin' his face when I jumped him in that old adobe. Can't last in the Rangers much longer. Just followin' all leads and crossin' my fingers.'

'You got an official dodger out on this feller?'

Parry hesitated, pursed his lips, shook his head.

'Fact is, no. Like I said, can't be *sure* he's the one, but I'd like to get him in and talk with him. Heard he went down to Mexico but figured I'd check around first.'

Garner looked pointedly at Parry's straightened leg. 'Can't see you traipsin' all the way down to *mañana* land with that leg.'

The Ranger's eye narrowed.

'No. Look, you hear of anyone usin' that name, you get in touch, OK?' He pulled out a leather-bound notebook, tore out a page. 'That's the small spread I aim to retire to. Just south of Fort Worth. You send me a wire an' I'll pay for it and git on down here somehow. Don't matter if it takes years, you hear about this Dallas, I want to know about it.'

Garner promised he would let him know; it would cost nothing. He tossed the piece of notepaper into a drawer and promptly forgot about it.

It was only later that he had come across the name: Dallas Marchant had registered for prove-up on a quarter-section on Comanche Creek, with his new young wife, Carrie. But, by then, Dallas had been and gone, to Mexico or to hell, no one knew and Garner had no interest.

Now, with Tag Daybright breathing down his neck, he knew he had to do something – leastways, be *seen* to be doing something.

So he rummaged around in his drawer amongst the dust-balls and fluff and odds and ends he hadn't cleaned out since taking office – and located the faded, crumpled notepaper Parry had given him.

The old Ranger would have retired years ago, might've even died, but he had nothing to lose by sending him a wire. At least he could tell Daybright what Parry had told him – not mentioning, of course, that it wasn't certain that 'Dallas' was this outlaw named 'Texas'.

If he got a reply from Parry, fine. If not he would still have *something* to tell Tag Daybright – and, he hoped, get him off his back.

Jed Handley and Ray Morgan watched warily as Whipple took his bottle of whiskey and glass to a corner table and sat down with his back to the wall, one boot up on the spare chair. Not that anyone would have been loco enough to wander up and sit down uninvited, mind. Whipple would as soon shoot your kneecap off as not.

It was plain he didn't want company – and that was

OK with Morg and Jed. They tried to stay inconspic-
uous as they drank their beer at the far end of the
bar. Whipple's roving gaze passed over them but
without interest.

So they jumped when his voice snapped their
names. When they looked up, he lifted one hand and
crooked a finger. Hesitantly, watched by all the other
drinkers, they walked slowly towards the Top D
ramrod's table. Without preamble, Whipple said:

'This Dallas give any hint *why* he wanted to work
for the Lindons?'

Jed was the one under Whip's gaze and he licked
his tongue, shook his head.

'Nary a thing, Whip.'

Whipple's eyes slid to Morgan. The man shook his
head, then frowned and said slowly:

'Never said why he wanted to work there but – Jed,
you recollect he said somethin' about the land across
the crick? Somethin' like, as if he was talkin' to
himself almost. "Be good lookin' out on the old
place again." You recollect that?'

Jed frowned and then nodded.

'By hell, yeah! He did say that. We wondered what
he meant. But he still didn't say why he wanted to
sign on with Lindon.'

'Just had you fellers roust him and then rode in
like a hero. . . .' Whip nodded. 'All right. Get away
from me.'

They went back to their beers and Whipple left
soon after. They breathed more easily and then
Morgan said:

'Wonder why Dallas *did* want to set that up so

Lindon would hire him? I mean, he went to a deal of trouble. Cost him eighty bucks which ain't hay. 'Stead of movin' on as we figured, mebbe we oughta stay put and see if we can cut ourselves in on whatever it is?'

Jed frowned. 'Might be we could kinda hit him for a grubstake. Say we could go tell Lindon all about the set-up unless Dallas paid us to keep quiet. . . ?'

Morg ran a tongue around his lips but grinned.

'It gives me a bellyful of snakes thinkin' about it but – why the hell not?'

They ordered another beer each on the strength of their decision.

Dallas was straddling the top corral post, rolling a cigarette, when Corey Lindon came out, with a glass of lemonade sent by Jemma.

Dallas nodded his thanks, finished rolling his cigarette and stuck it behind his ear while he sipped the drink. He gestured to distant hills across Comanche Creek.

'See dust up there. Lot of riders.'

Lindon nodded.

'Be Daybright's men. Roundin' up mavericks.'

'Starting early.'

Lindon smiled wryly.

'Tag always gets pick of the bunch – in anythin'.'

Dallas looked around the yard.

'We've a lot of work to get done round here, finish the barn, dig a root cellar, maybe another well. But we could take time out to get you some mavericks before Daybright takes 'em all.'

Lindon seemed startled.

'But – well, I don't know anythin' about chasin' wild cows! I've only had experience with milkers.'

He indicated the two Jersey cows chomping their cuds in the shade of a lean-to where they were milked night and morning.

'This is good land. You'll grow fine crops – but there's a lot of graze you can put to use, too. If there're mavericks loose in the hills, be plumb loco not to go after your share.'

'I – we weren't really thinking of raising cattle for meat – not for a few years.'

'Help you get established sooner. Crops are OK but they take time and a lot depends on the weather. You get some beef herds started and it counts for a lot with the Land Agency. No outlay except a little sweat. We've got the fences up now. Be the right time to start a small herd.'

Lindon glanced worriedly towards the hills where the dust clouds were plainly visible.

'But – if I run into Daybright's men . . .'

'Let me worry about that.'

He could see that the homesteader *wanted* to agree, obviously liked the idea of running his own herd, but was afraid to take that first step.

'Tell you what. I know those hills a little. Was up this way some years back. What say I ride up and take a look around? I'll stay clear of Top D riders. I'm not going looking for trouble, but . . .'

'You won't duck it.'

Dallas smiled thinly.

'Not my way. No, I'll scout around, maybe manage

to throw a loop over a few mavericks, come back in a couple days and let you know the lie of the land. It's an opportunity you oughtn't to miss out on, Corey.'

Lindon glanced towards the cabin, where Jemma was no doubt cooking or sewing, teeth tugging at his bottom lip.

'I – I should come with you.'

'Not this time. Let me see how things are back in those hills and if I can see a way for you to get yourself a small herd, why we'll go get it. Meantime, you figure out what brand you want to burn into the critters' hides. OK?'

Lindon stared up at him soberly.

'Sometimes I wonder who's workin' for who round here.'

Dallas grinned, took his cigarette from behind his ear and lit up.

'Just making suggestions – boss.'

Lindon smiled, a little embarrassed. 'Sorry – I – I know I'm a rank greenhorn. It – rubs me the wrong way sometimes because I know so little. Dallas, I think yours is a good idea. I'll go have Jemma pack you a grubsack while you saddle your horse.'

Dallas jumped down.

'There you are – making your own decisions. You're the boss, Corey. Don't let me bully you. It's just that I've been pushed around some these last few years and I can get a mite bossy myself at times. You rein me in when I do.'

Lindon smiled, took the empty glass and was whistling softly as he started back towards the cabin, calling to Jemma.

He paused and looked around with a jerky movement.

'Dallas – why're you doin' this?' At Dallas's blank stare he added: 'You know – you've kind of – adopted us. Why're you lookin' out for Jem and me?'

Dallas shrugged, keeping his face sober.

'Maybe I see in you something I once had myself. I had no one to help me, thought I could do it all alone. Instead – well, it didn't work out. In the worst possible way.'

'That's – your explanation?'

'Only one I've got for now.'

Lindon held his gaze a moment longer, nodded slowly, and then continued on his way up to the cabin, obviously deep in thought.

Dallas swore softly as he shook out his rope.

CHAPTER 7

ROUND-UP

There were at least five Top D men in the hills. They had taken over a box canyon where they had built a brush fence across the entrance and kept their rounded-up mavericks in there.

Dallas watched from a ridge, careful to shade the lenses of his field glasses so the sun wouldn't flash from them. He recognized one of the men he had laid out when he had first asked Tag Daybright for a job: Curly, he thought the man's name was. The rest were strangers, but that was to be expected.

He worked his way back into the shadow of the big boulder, absently cleaned the lenses with the tail of his shirt. By a rough count, Top D had already brought in close to seventy head. Looking at the country and the brush and general lay-but, Dallas figured there wouldn't be a lot more here. Seventy was a really good bunch and their bawling and snorting and the dull crashes as the more frustrated ones butted into the brush fence, filled this part of the hills.

He glanced up at the sun. Three or four hours yet to sundown but the Top D riders looked as though they were calling it a day. They were lounging about the camp area, passing round a bottle of something – maybe moonshine whipped up by one of the cowboys on the sly – rolling cigarettes, talking and laughing among themselves.

Dallas climbed down to where he had left his horse, mounted and rode quietly away, turned and headed back into the hills proper. Spoor was easy enough to find. He backtracked to where they had driven down the mavericks, saw where it was leading: into thicker brush choking a valley between the hills that wasn't readily discernible from down by Comanche Creek. These cowboys would know this country well, of course, better than he did.

He had been here before, but that was years ago, and he hadn't really done much exploring. There had been too much to do around the quarter-section, readying it so that it had the appearance of work done by a man who aimed to make his prove-up time-limit – with nothing else on his mind.

Well, that had been then – this was now. And he still had the same thing on his mind as he'd had then. But he wasn't so sure about it now: a lot of things had changed since he had ridden down to Mexico with Hansen and the others. During all those terrible years in Black Hell he had often thought of the irony of life. Fact was, he hadn't *needed* to join that wild bunch, planning the raid on the Mexican cattle herds. But he had gone so no one would be suspicious: if he hadn't agreed to ride with them they would have wondered why. Outwardly, he needed a break like all of them, money was short, time was running out. Rustling a few hundred head of Mexican cattle would give them all a good start towards prove-up.

But he hadn't really needed that! That was the big joke life had played on him. He had only gone with the others so no one would suspect he had . . . other sources for helping him meet the prove-up time-limit. Even now, riding through this brush-choked valley, years down the trail, hundreds of miles from Black Hell, his smile was bitter.

He was back but the land was gone, now part of Top D, and it didn't even look the same. He couldn't even find the grave on a quick look around, but maybe it was still there and just needed closer inspection.

And he no longer had to prove-up, no longer even had a wife to provide for. . . .

He had thought it would be easy once he realized he had survived the break-out from the Black Hell. Ride back to Comanche Creek and – take it from there.

'Not quite that easy, *amigo*,' he said aloud. 'Nothing is ever quite that easy for you.'

He saw cattle, higher up, brush-poppers, no doubt watching him warily as he approached. They disappeared into the thick brush and their hidden by-ways but he saw their sign. Grown steers, and once he got close enough to see the brand on the rump: Top D.

Another, twenty minutes later, showed as Cross N, two uprights with an 'X' linking them. That would be Nolan's place, downstream beyond the homesteaders.

It wasn't a good sign. It meant that the ranchers could – and would – claim the mavericks belonged to them, offspring of their cattle. Many a man had died trying to keep mavericks under such circumstances. But others had fought back, if not with guns, in the courts. Sometimes they had won.

He couldn't see the Lindons taking either Daybright or Bix Nolan to court and walking away winners. Cattle-country judges hardly ever favoured homesteaders in their decisions. So, the only way to hold on to any mavericks gathered was by the gun.

And that was right in his line. . . .

He camped cold that night, waited until the stars told him it was after ten o'clock and the moon was just starting to rise. Then he made his way back to the box canyon where Top D had their mavericks.

As he suspected, all five of the cowhands were asleep, snoring. Two empty bottles reflected the coals of the dying camp-fire. He rode his horse down on the grassy slope, dismounted by some boulders and made his way to the brush fence. The mavericks were tolerably quiet, still a few bawling, one or two stubborn ones still trying to bust a way out.

He helped them.

He tore away the brush on his side, weakening the fence. The mavericks soon realized it and within minutes the first few had shouldered a way through.

They bawled exuberantly, trumpeting through the night, sending their message back to those still inside the canyon.

The fence collapsed under the press of eager, escaping mavericks and he stood to one side, waving his hat, slapping it against his legs and the rocks, driving them away from his position, towards the downslope. They veered and went down and he leapt into the saddle, putting his mount into their midst, cutting off a slice of the heaving, jostling herd. The majority of the mavericks surged over towards the cowboys' camp and he heard the startled yells and curses as half-awake rannies scrambled to get out of the way.

Dallas figured he had fifteen or more head and he hazed them hard with the sweating horse, yanking it this way and that, keeping them bunched as well as he could.

The camp above was in chaos and he knew the cowpokes would be too blame busy to even see this breakaway bunch. He had selected his place during late afternoon, guided the small herd down into the dry wash where they had no choice but to follow its meanderings. Then, at the end, he cut in fast, slapping with his hat, leaning from the saddle, kicking at dusty hides, boot-toe driving hard behind laid-back ears of the leaders.

They veered, snorting, complaining, but wanting only to get away from this harassing son of a bitch on the horse. He drove them into a brush-choked funnel, the bushes acting as a guide, through to a tight pass that was no more than a broken cleft in the rocks, slowing them down. But they picked their way through and he was waiting for them, galloped in with swinging rope, yelling madly now.

Just after midnight, he hazed nineteen mavericks on to Lindon's quarter-section, replaced the rails in the fence, which he had dropped earlier, and washed the dust from his throat with tepid water from his canteen.

The mavericks were quieter now, in open graze, with water trickling and tinkling through the night only yards away. They soon settled down.

And Dallas was up and cooking breakfast in his battered skillet when the first of the Top D riders showed up on the far side of the fence in the grey light.

He turned and nodded.

'Must've smelled my bacon. But you're out of luck, fellers. I'm just cooking the last of it.'

'It could be the last of any meal for you, mister!' growled a squat man with a big hat that sat like a cart-wheel on his head and shaded his face.

'Why's that?'

The man gestured.

'Them mavericks. They belong to Top D.'

'Friend, mavericks belong to the man who rounds 'em up.'

'They still belong to Top D. We rounded up them mavericks yest'y. Them and fifty others.'

'You're mistaken. I hazed this here bunch in here myself not four, five hours ago.'

'In the middle of the night!'

Dallas shrugged, forking up some limp bacon and

dropping it on to a grease-fried biscuit.

'Man, I don't look a gift horse in the mouth. They come right up to my fence, bustin' to get in. Happened I had some rails down for repair and they came on through and I hazed 'em on to the grass. Never seen any others, but I got them rails back in place, pronto.'

'We had nigh on seventy in a box canyon. They busted out, scattered to hell an' gone through the hills.'

Dallas, munching, stood up shaking his head.

'If you're stupid enough not to ride herd on your catch, mister, you deserve to lose the lot.'

The men growled and moved uneasily. Curly was there and he might be remembering the way Dallas had gun-whipped him so easily that day at Top D headquarters, for he said to the squat man:

'He ain't afraid, Frog. He'll face us all down if we push it.'

Frog scowled at Curly.

'Five against one? No one's that good. Look, you, Dallas or whatever your name is, we want them mavericks and we're gonna take 'em! You want to take us all on, you're loco, but we'll oblige!'

'Damn you, Frog!' Dallas said, dropping his half-eaten biscuit. 'I ain't a morning person and I like my breakfast nice and quiet. Now git before I shoot you out from under that silly-looking hat.'

The insult about the hat seemed to do it. Frog let out a cuss, said:

'Teach the son of a bitch a lesson, boys!' and reached for his gun.

The others – except for Curly who backed his horse away quickly, went for their guns, too, some reaching for their saddle rifles, others for their six-guns.

They were all way too slow.

Dallas's right hand dipped and came up with Peacemaker blazing. Frog somersaulted backwards over his horse. The man next to him grabbed at his forearm as his rifle clattered to the ground. Next man along had his Colt up and half-cocked when a bullet knocked him out of the saddle. The fourth man literally threw his rifle away from him, frantically reaching for handfuls of air.

A bullet punched through one of those hands and he snatched it back, hugging it across his chest as blood spurted.

Curly was riding hell for leather across the creek, heading for the brush.

Dallas, Peacemaker holstered now, working the lever on his Winchester, walked across to the fence and placed a boot on the bottom rail. He ignored the two nursing wounds in their saddles and looked at Frog and the other downed man. Frog had a head wound, bleeding, no doubt making his ears ring as he sat there, shaking his head from side to side. The other man clasped his shoulder, blood trickling through his fingers.

'Go tell Daybright you lost some mavericks to me. Tell him *you* lost 'em because you didn't set a nighthawk watching your herd. Tell him he tries to take these off me, he'll be in a helluva lot of trouble. They'll be branded in an hour – and if that don't stop him, I will.'

'You're – dead!' gasped Frog but Dallas merely turned his back, walked back to his fire and dug out the last strip of bacon, now shrivelled and blackened, from the skillet, swore as he wrapped it in a greasy biscuit. He hunkered down, chewing, made coffee, and watched the Top D men slowly gather themselves and ride away.

Lindon had decided to call his spread the 'JL'. It was an easy brand to make into an iron. The mavericks weren't branded within the hour, but they were before the second hour was up.

Corey Lindon stood up stiffly, blotting sweat from his face, flushed and excited after the busy, physical effort of branding the reluctant mavericks. He grinned through the dirt and sweat as he placed his hands on his hips and looked at the scattered cows, some grazing, others trying to lick their stinging brands.

'Dallas, I'm sure glad you stopped by. I feel like I'm gettin' somewhere at last!'

'Sure, you've got your first herd started. Ride into town and register your brand and no one can cause you trouble then.'

Lindon sobered, looking at him steadily.

'You didn't explain that shooting I heard just after daybreak.'

'Told you, there was a little problem but it's fixed now. When you go into town, see Shackleton for a couple rolls of that barbed wire. Reckon we could put it to good use.'

Lindon frowned.

'I – don't think so. I'm sure Daybright would see that as – provocative.' He held up a hand. 'No argument, Dallas. That's my decision.'

Dallas's face was impassive for a short time. Then he smiled slowly.

'You're the boss,' he said.

Tag Daybright turned from pacing across his room and stood glaring at the hangdog Frog who was managing to moan convincingly every so often and wince, putting a hand to the crude bandage around his head, reminding his boss he had been wounded fighting for what was rightfully Top D's.

Tag pointed a stiff finger at him.

'You let Dallas steal my cows!'

Frog shook his head quickly, and the wince was genuine this time: his brain felt loose in his skull.

'We called him out, boss! Never figured he'd take on five of us. Well, four, really, 'cos Curly rode off.'

Daybright curled a lip.

'I'll see him later. *Four* of you and Dallas still outgunned you!'

'Boss, I – I never seen anyone use a gun so fast! Truth is, I never even seen him draw. One minute he's standin' there, next there's a blazin' gun in his fist and we're bein' blown outta the saddle. Reckon he could've killed us all if he'd a mind.'

Daybright's frown deepened.

'Ye-ah. Sounds dangerous. If that damn sheriff had found out somethin' about his past . . . well, all right. So he took twenty mavericks from us. Plenty more in the hills if you know where to look.' He leaned his fists on the desk edge. 'You – go – look! And take all them rannies was with you before. You men are gonna learn that when I give you a job to do, I expect it to be done. Properly!'

Frog moaned but stifled it quickly at the look on Tag's rugged face.

'You could get Garner to charge him, boss.'

Tag snorted. 'You already told me any tracks he might've left were overlaid by the mavericks. You never actually *saw* him run them on to Lindon's place. I'd make a fool of myself, look like a damn whinin' nester, runnin' to the law, even if I do own a piece of it.'

'You can't let him get away with it!'

The words burst spontaneously out of Frog and he cringed when he realized how he had spoken to Daybright. But, surprisingly, Daybright just shook his head.

'He won't get away with it. Nor will Lindon. Somethin's goin' on there and I aim to get it in my sights before I start chargin' in and maybe ride into a bullet. Send in Whip. Then get back to the hills and throw a loop on every damn maverick you can find!'

Frog shuffled out and Tag poured himself a drink.

He was annoyed as hell to find his hand shaking so much that he spilled some of the liquor.

This kind of thing with the mavericks and Dallas – or Lindon, when you got right down to it – was a burr under his saddle, but the dam was what bothered him most. He was going to throw up a dam on his property which would put him in control of the water

84

in Comanche Creek, and so affect every home-
steader and rancher downstream.

Bix Nolan wasn't happy that Daybright would be
more or less controlling the flow of water, but Nolan
could be brought around – or, at a pinch, crushed. It
was the homesteaders who bothered Daybright most.
Not that they were powerful enough, even if they
banded together, to give him much trouble.

But their land was still under Federal jurisdiction
and so he would have to convince Washington that
his intentions were of the best in building the dam.
It meant he had to have a law-abiding reputation: if
there was any hint that he was against the homesteaders they wouldn't let him build the dam. Of
course, he could simply throw it up on his own land,
but a few complaints by the likes of Lindon or
Hanrahan or others downstream, that he was cutting
their water supply, and the Federals would slap a
charge on him and he could end up in jail or be hit
with a mighty big fine.

It was this fear of crossing swords with the Federal
people that had held him back so far. He had
managed to come out of it looking clean when his
men had been accused of harassing the nesters: he
had fired them and, quietly, using other names, had
set them up on prove-up sections that he would later
buy from them and add to Top D. *Legally.*

But the damn Feds were tying his hands! And he
couldn't shake the feeling that this Dallas's appearance wasn't just coincidental. According to the
survey map he had once tried to prove-up on land
now belonging to Top D. A man with that kind of

ready-made knowledge would be of value to anyone who might want to know more about what was really happening out at Comanche Creek. And he had rigged things so as to get that job with the Lindons. *If only he knew Dallas's background!*

He might be working undercover for the Feds, a US marshal, maybe, or someone hired by the Land Agency.

He downed his drink and was pouring another when Whipple came in, still showing plenty of signs of his losing fight with Dallas. Tag smiled crookedly and poured another glass, offering it to the battered ramrod.

'How'd you like a chance to square things with Dallas, Whip, old *amigo*. . . ? I mean, *really* square things with the son of a bitch. Put him outta the picture permanently.'

Whipple took the glass and lifted it, smiling crookedly.

'I'll drink to that!'

CHAPTER 8

KILLER

While Corey Lindon was away in town registering his new JL brand – Jemma going with him – Dallas figured it was as good a time as any to take a look around the old quarter-section he had filed on eight years earlier. And subsequently lost when he took that fateful ride down to Mexico.

The cows – no longer 'mavericks' now they were branded – seemed content enough to browse on the grass along the banks of the creek. Dallas was supposed to be working on the barn but, as Lindon had said he and Jemma wouldn't be back until around sundown, he figured he could take a little time off to do something for himself.

He sat his horse under some shade trees and smoked down a full cigarette, watching Top D land closely. He saw riders, but they were not working the creek, nor the timber close down to the Lindon place. Mostly they were back in the hills, dust rising from where he had first seen it yesterday when Frog and his men had been chousing mavericks out of the brush. *Looking for more mavericks.* They would know the cunning old cows' hiding-places for their offspring and would likely make up for the nineteen head he had grabbed.

Good. That would keep them busy, and there were the remainder of the other mavericks to be rounded up after the breakout from the box canyon. These same animals would have to be branded with the Top D sign, so he ought to have this section of Daybright's spread all to himself for a while.

He dropped a rail off the panel of fence that had been designed for access, stepped his mount across and replaced the rail. Riding warily, watching the hills and draws and timber constantly, he rode out on to this land that he and Carrie had pinned their hopes on all those years ago.

He had expected to see the remains of the log cabin, if not tumbled down in ruins, then maybe still standing and put to use by Daybright's crew. But there was nothing in the place where he figured it ought to be. *The whole damn face of the land had changed!*

A little casual questioning had earned him the information from Lindon that there had been a big flash flood last year.

'Kind of prone to flooding, the old Comanche, when there's been a lot of rain back in the hills,' Lindon had explained. 'Seems there was a big land-slide up there that kind of changed the course of the creek, narrowed it so it shoots out like soda-pop from

a bottle and sends a wall of water down here, tearin'
away the banks and everythin'.'

That explained it: the creek hadn't been prone to
much flooding when Dallas and Carrie had been
working this section.

So that would be how come there was little to see
where the original cabin had stood. Searching
around brought him to the place and he saw a few
signs of the foundations, noting that much of the
small rise where he had built the cabin had been
washed away completely.

His mouth tightened: it was going to be harder
than ever to locate the grave.

Having found the cabin site, he tried to find his
landmarks but trees had been washed away, a big
clump of boulders distributed across the ground like
a kid's scattered marbles. He remembered he had
dug the grave just to the south of those rocks, figur-
ing they would offer some protection from the bleak
winds that roared through in winter – which was
when he had laid away that dying Yankee in the
unmarked grave. At that time, he hadn't aimed to
advertise its location to anyone – not even Carrie.
Not for a while. . . .

Now he took bearings as well as he could and he
knew he couldn't change what his search was telling
him: that the grave itself was now beneath two of the
largest boulders that had been moved by the flood
waters.

Two huge chunks of granite, resting right where
he was now sure the grave was, each weighing a
couple of tons.

It would take dynamite to shift them – and the explosion was bound to destroy the grave itself. *Dammittohell!*

He was working on the barn when he heard riders coming into the yard. Dallas had a mouthful of nails, ready to drive them into an upright he had checked out with a chisel and saw, but now he spat the nails into his cupped hand when he recognized the new arrivals.

Jed Handley and Ray Morgan. They were looking around the yard rather tensely, then dismounted slowly.

'You there, Dallas?' Morgan called.

He jumped when Dallas appeared from behind some stacked planking ready for the barn's frame. There were no tools in his hands now and they saw that his right hand was close to the butt of the holstered Peacemaker.

'What d'you two want? Thought I told you I didn't want to see you again.'

Jed held up a hand, licking his lips.

'Well, we got somethin' to tell you and when we seen Lindon and his missus in town for a day's shoppin', figured this was a good time.'

'Meeting with you two is never a good time. Say your piece and vamoose.'

Jed glanced at Morgan, who seemed content to let the other man do the talking. Handley cleared his throat.

'Well, it's this way. You hired us to roust the Lindons so's you could show up and "rescue" 'em, and get yourself a job. Which we did and which you did.'

'You were paid.'

'Sure. No complaints there . . .' He paused and swallowed before adding, 'But the money's gone. We're broke.'

Dallas said nothing, merely raked both men with his cold gaze. Jed nudged Morgan who spoke up harshly, obviously nervous.

'We figured you must've wanted this job mighty bad – for your own reasons. So – mebbe it's worth a little somethin' for us to keep our mouths shut and not tell Lindon about the deal you made with us.'

Dallas's hard expression didn't alter. He continued to stare and they moved uncomfortably, changing their weight from one foot to the other, scratching at sudden itches on their noses or jaws, lifting their hats and wiping forearms across sweating brows.

Dallas stayed silent.

'Well – what you say?' blurted Morgan suddenly.

'Ride on out.'

'Sure. With mebbe a hundred bucks?'

'With mebbe a whole skin. Stay to argue and you mightn't ride out at all. Or go toting some extra lead.'

Both men took involuntary steps backward but they had braced themselves to come out here now and they knew it was the one and only chance they would get. They were scared, tight-faced, pale, but they were determined, too, figured they held the upper hand.

'Hundred's a cheap price to pay for us keepin' quiet,' Jed croaked. 'We ride out and you go about whatever business you got in mind.'

'Sure. You ride out. Then when you booze or piss away that hundred, you come back again.' Dallas shook his head slowly. 'Ride out now while you can and count your lucky stars.'

Suddenly, Morgan smiled crookedly.

'We ride out now, we're likely to come across the Lindons on the trail out from town. Or we could wait until they come along and . . . have a talk with 'em.'

'Uh-huh,' Dallas said slowly, eyes narrowing. 'Thanks for reminding me, Morg. Can't let that happen.'

'Judas!' breathed Jed, sweating profusely now, glaring at Morg. 'Why'd you have to open your big mouth! Now he won't let us ride out at all!'

Morg realized his mistake but it was way too late now – and he knew Jed spoke gospel. The look on Dallas's face said it all: they were a danger to him as long as they were alive. So . . .

With a small, strangled cry, Morg suddenly thrust his pard away from him, hoping to distract Dallas, and drove down for his six-gun.

Dallas's shot crashed out through the afternoon and Morgan spun half-way around, his gun falling from his hand as it barely cleared leather. Then his legs folded and he sprawled on his face, one leg twitching.

Handley had backed up, lifted both hands in front of his face, half-cringing.

'Don't! I won't say nothin'! I – I'll ride clear outta the county. I swear!'

Dallas was covering him with the smoking gun and he stared at the man for a long, terrifying moment, and then said curtly,

'Take Morg and bury him somewhere a long way from here. I see you again, Jed, I'll shoot you on sight.'

Handley had no argument with that. Under Dallas's cold gaze he struggled and panted and eventually got his dead pard over his horse, roped him on loosely, then mounted warily, watching Dallas all the time.

He rode out, looking around constantly, shoulders hunched as if he was expecting a bullet to slam into them at any moment.

Dallas watched him off the land and then went back to his barn-building, pausing just long enough to kick some dirt over a bloodstain on the ground where Morg had fallen.

'What the hell d'you think you're at?'

Jed Handley's heart almost stopped. He spun around from stacking the first few rocks over Morg's stretched-out body and felt his bowels quake.

Whip Whipple was standing on the rock above him, covering him casually with his rifle.

'Judas, Whip! You like to gimme a heart attack!'

'What you done? Boozed-up, have a fallin'-out with Morg an' shoot him?'

'No! No! Judas, I din' kill him. Was that Dallas. I swear.'

Whipple smiled crookedly.

'Sure. I believe you. Hundreds wouldn't. So mebbe you better tell me your story.'

He climbed down carefully, waving the rifle at Jed so that the man stepped back, making no movements that could get him into more trouble than he was already in. When Whip stood before him, glancing down at Morg's body, Jed said:

'Damn fool tried to out-draw Dallas. He never had a chance.'

'And you? How come he left you alive?'

'Told me to ride out and bury Morg. That if he seen me again he'd shoot on sight.'

'What'd you do to upset him?'

'Nothin'!' protested Jed, but when he saw the tightening of Whip's cut and swollen mouth, heard the clash of the rifle lever, he lifted his hands quickly. 'All right, all right! Me and Morg figured to hit Dallas for some more dinero. Said we'd tell Lindon about the way he rigged things so's he could get taken on as a ranch hand.'

Whipple nodded.

'Always knew you two were stupid. Where'd it happen?'

'Lindon's. We seen Dallas come back from Top D, waited a spell and rode in.' Jed told the full story, seeing no point in hiding anything now. When he had finished, Whip leaned his rifle against a rock, rolled a thick cigarette and fired up. He flicked the dead vesta at Jed and the man jumped back. Whip laughed briefly. *What was Dallas doing sneaking around on Top D land?* Whip wondered, but said aloud:

94

'And he called you, huh?'

'Yeah. I'm tellin' you, Whip, I'm scared. He's a killer, that Dallas.'

'Seems so.' He smoked thoughtfully. Tag had offered him $200 to go after Dallas, make it personal, use the fight as an excuse for squaring things.

'You kill him any way you want, but you don't say I paid you to do it.' Tag had told him. 'It was all your idea. Two hundred and I'll set you up on that quarter-section on Piney Knoll, give you a coupla hands to help you prove-up, then buy it back off you. And by that time, I might even be able to hire you on again at Top D.'

Whip was against it at first. Oh, sure, he wanted to nail Dallas so bad it was keeping him awake at night, but he didn't care for losing his job. Garner would bitch but he would do what Daybright told him in the end and put it down to self-defence and a private quarrel. But – well, Whipple liked the way he could lord it over not only the ranch hands but just about everybody on the high plains *because* he was Daybright's ramrod. Still, it would be easy working that quarter-section on Piney Knoll with a couple of hands to do the hard chores . . . and money in his pocket afterwards.

But he would still prefer to be on Top D's payroll as ramrod and Tag Daybright's troubleshooter. He liked the way men stepped around him because of that.

And just when he had smoked down his cigarette and started to build another, the idea came to him.

He lit the new smoke, glanced at Jed, who seemed

afraid to make any kind of a move or even to speak. Casually, Whip picked up his rifle and cradled it across his chest, the burning cigarette hanging from his lower lip.

'Jed, you might's well bury Morg, I guess, and move on. Nothin' for you around here. . . . Dallas likely meant what he said about shootin' you on sight. . . .'

'Hell, I know he did, Whip! Sooner I get outta here the better.'

Whipple nodded. 'Yeah. Well, you cover up Morg and I'll ride with you to the edge of the hills, see you clear the county safely.'

'You'd do that for me, Whip? That's mighty white of you.'

'Any enemy of Dallas is a friend of mine,' Whip said, smiling as Jed turned away to look for more rocks.

Then the rifle swung up and he shot Handley in the back, the bullet shattering the man's spine.

'Well, Dallas, you sure been a naughty boy – ain't you.'

Whip's guffaw scared a brace of birds high in a red oak and they took off with screeches and a shower of leaves drifting groundwards.

CHAPTER 9

DEPUTY

Otis Garner was suspicious of Whipple's story but there was no way he could disprove it.

'And Jed Handley *told* you Dallas had shot him and Morgan?' he asked again and saw the tightening of Whipple's battered, impatient face.

'How many damn times, Otis? I found 'em along the trail, Morgan already dead, Jed close to breathin' his last. He said Dallas had bushwhacked 'em, nailed Morg dead centre and when Jed tried to run, got him in the back.'

Garner scratched at his face.

'Only thing is, Whip, I seen that wound in Jed. It busted his spine. Like to kill a man between breaths, a shot like that.'

'I've seen that happen,' Whipple conceded, 'but Jed was still alive when I found him – only just, but still with enough breath to name his killer.' Whipple rolled another cigarette, lit it from the burning butt of his previous one and stomped this out on the sheriff's floor, ignoring Garner's scowl. He moved closer to the desk.

'What I want you to do, Otis, is deputize me so I can go hunt down this Dallas – all legitimate, like. A killer on the loose . . .' He shrugged. 'Kinda man anyone'd shoot on sight. If I've got a badge to back it up, why, hell, I've done my duty, huh? And you've done yours, by sendin' a man out to do a job he's better at than you are.'

Garner flushed, mighty wary now.

'Tag wants you to do this?'

'He wants Dallas out of it – all above board. Wants me to do it because I've got a personal grudge agin the son of a bitch. That's OK, but we do it this way, I'm better off. You don't need to know the details. Just gimme a badge.'

'I dunno about this, Whip,' Garner said slowly, sitting back in his chair. 'I just – dunno.'

'What's to know? You'll be doin' Tag a favour and no one can have too many of them to their credit.'

'Thing is, there's a Ranger on his way.'

Whip stepped back quickly. 'A *Ranger*!'

'Well, he's kinda retired now but he's got a mighty good reputation. Likely you've heard of him. Jubal Parry.'

Whip swore.

'Hell, he's *old*. A cripple I heard. Why the hell's he buyin' in?'

Garner scratched the side of his face again.

'He's been lookin' for Dallas for years. When you said Tag wanted any old dodgers that might be out on him, I got in touch with Parry, figurin' he'd know more about him than anyone else.' He lifted a yellow telegram-form from his desk. 'Just got his wire to say he's comin' on down. I make you a deputy and – well, I dunno, Whip. . . .'

'If I nail Dallas before he gets here, what's his beef? I'll be doin' him a favour. Be doin' *everyone* a favour. Specially Tag. . . .'

'Well – I kinda think Parry'd like to do it himself. He blames Dallas for his crippled hip, claims he shot him there.'

Whipple shook his head.

'Forget the damn Ranger! Tag wants it done quick. Now you can butter up this old crippled coot, who can't do a damn thing for you, Otis, or you can gimme that deputy's badge and Tag'll look after you. Now you're a damn fool in my book in lots of ways, but you ain't *that* big a fool – are you?'

When Whipple had ridden in with the two dead hardcases roped over a horse, the town, of course, had stopped in its tracks and followed him down to the law office. Quite a few men hung around even after Sheriff Garner had told them to disperse before he started running folk in.

These men were crowded close to the closed door and Beebe Biddle, having the best hearing, kept an ear against the panel and conveyed the conversation inside to the small group of stickybeaks gathered around him.

So the word soon spread through the town: Dallas had bushwhacked Jed Handley and Ray Morgan and now Whip Whipple had been made a deputy and was readying for a long trail, going after Dallas with a 'dead-or-alive' sanction from Garner.

Jemma Lindon was just collecting a length of cloth which she planned to make into a new dress when the other women in the store crowded around Mrs Longley, a sharp-nosed gossip – actually the biggest gossip in town, sharp-nosed or otherwise. She told the full story with relish.

Alarmed, but not noticed by the others who were plying Mrs Longley for even more details, Jemma hurried out of the store and trotted along the street until she found her husband behind the livery, dickering over the price of a spotted dun gelding he was interested in. He was just closing the deal in his favour when Jemma appeared and made it plain she had to see him urgently. He swore softly – he hadn't wanted the hostler to draw breath on his final spiel – but he sighed and took Jemma's arm, urged her to one side.

'Jem! I've almost got that geldin' for my price. What the devil is it that's so important?'

His face straightened when she told him, finishing with:

'Whipple's been deputized – so it'll be a legitimate killing! We have to do something, Corey! We have to warn Dallas!'

He was reluctant, but Corey Lindon was essentially a decent man and he knew he owed Dallas that much, at least – and a lot more. He turned to the rat-faced hostler.

'All right, Caleb. Your price, *if* you throw in the

bridle and that old saddle.'

'Done!' the hostler agreed readily and Lindon knew immediately he had paid too much. But it was done now, the handshakes given. . . .

While Caleb saddled the horse, Corey urged Jemma towards the big livery doors.

'You'll have to drive the buckboard back. Will you be all right?'

'Of course. Are you—'

He nodded, chopping off her words.

'Yeah. I'll cut across country, start right away. I ought to be able to warn Dallas in time.'

As he turned away, she placed a hand on his forearm, pale now.

'Corey – please be careful. Whipple's a killer.' She paused and added quietly: 'You don't think Dallas did ambush those two men, do you?'

Tight-faced, Lindon said:

'I dunno what to think, except we can't let Whipple kill Dallas.' He turned to lend Caleb a hand. His mouth was dry and his hands were already shaking.

But he would make his ride to warn Dallas, come hell or high water.

He even felt a small surge of pride as he spurred the gelding through the open doors and waved briefly at Jemma as she hurried along the boardwalk, the parcel under her arm almost forgotten in her concern for Dallas – and her husband.

Dallas was back mending the barn when he heard Corey Lindon calling his name. The man was just riding a lathered dun Dallas had never, seen before into the yard, calling hoarsely.

'What's the hurry?' Dallas called, tools in hand, but belly tightening at the obvious near-panic driving Lindon. He immediately thought something must have happened to the woman.

Lindon tried to slip saddle before the horse had stopped skidding but he wasn't that good. He sprawled and tumbled in the gravel. Dallas hauled him to his feet and looked into the flushed, excited face.

'Comanche break-out or something?'

Lindon shook his head, swallowing, trying to moisten his dry mouth with spittle.

'Wh- Whipple! Comin' – after – you.'

Dallas's gaze instinctively lifted past his boss. He raked it over the countryside but there was no sign of any other rider.

'Well, I guess he figures he needs to square things . . .'

Lindon nodded jerkily, put a hand on Dallas's forearm.

'Daybright wants you dead but doesn't want it laid at his door. Whipple's gonna do it – and he's had Garner deputize him.'

'Hell! How'd he do that?'

Lindon slowed, watching Dallas's face.

'Claims you ambushed Morgan and Jed Handley . . .'

'No. They braced me just after I got back from looking around my old quarter-section . . .' He saw the start Lindon gave and added with a crooked

102

smile, jerking his head towards the fence line, south of the timber fence. 'Yeah – that's it, just across there.'

'You never said – you said you'd tried to prove-up on land *around* here but not right next door . . .'

'Never mind that. Those two dead-beats braced me and I had to kill Morgan. Handley rode out with him. I told him to bury him along the trail and then to clear the country or next time I saw him I'd shoot first and ask questions afterwards.'

Breath hissed through Corey Lindon's nose and he looked around tensely.

'You don't have a lot of time. I cut across country but I saw Whipple's dust in the pass. He brought Handley and Morgan in – both dead. Handley shot in the back. Said he found 'em along the trail and Handley said you'd done it.'

'Son of a bitch! He's framing me!'

'Well, he aims to kill you, whatever the straight of it, Dallas. You'd best head for the hills.'

Dallas's eyes flashed.

'I've done enough running in my life – from real lawmen.'

'Hell, man, you can't wait to shoot it out with him! He's a legal deputy now! Don't matter how he got the badge, it's legal and you kill a lawman . . .'

Dallas smiled wryly. 'I know all about that, Corey. Yeah, Daybright's made a smart move. Interesting to know why he wants me out of the way. Well, I won't bring down trouble on you, Corey, and I'm obliged for you warning me.'

He hadn't unsaddled his mount after riding back

from Top D and now he set his hat on squarely, checked his six-gun for loads, and started towards the corral fence where he had hitched the horse.

'There'll always be a place for you here, Dallas,' Corey told him, thrusting out his right hand.

Dallas took it, gripped briefly.

'I'll be on the run, but there's a place called Tower Hill where I can lie for Whip – and still keep an eye on things down here.'

'Thanks.' Corey watched him mount, stepped up to the horse and held the bridle lightly. 'Is there somethin' about that old ground you used to work, Dallas?' he asked shrewdly.

Dallas hesitated. 'There's a grave there . . .'

He said no more and Lindon nodded.

'Of sentimental value, you might say?'

'You might. *Adios*, Corey. Take care of Jemma now.'

Lindon watched him ride out of the yard and head for the hills, then turned slowly and walked across to the lathered dun, loosening the cinch strap and reaching down a burlap sack from the top corral rail to rub the animal down.

He stiffened.

There was a dust cloud from a hard-driving rider just swinging around the bend in the trail that led to the JL.

And Dallas was still in sight, climbing into the foothills.

Whipple saw him and as he lashed his hard-breathing mount to more speed, yelled at Lindon:

'I seen you in town! You warned him, din' you, you

son of a bitch! Well, I'll be back for you – *and* that good-lookin' missus of yours!'

Lindon felt the blood drain from his face as Whipple raced on across JL land.

Dallas remembered some of the hill trails from years ago but many of them had been altered by brush and timber growth so that he became lost and was stuck in the foothills for some time.

He paused under some trees, looking back down on to Lindon's land – and saw Whipple.

The man was making his way into the foothills already and Dallas's sharp eye saw that there was a double-barrelled sawn-off shotgun slung on the cantle as well as his rifle scabbard and whatever sidearms Whipple was wearing. There was a bulging grubsack, too, and two canteens. So Whipple was prepared for a long haul, it seemed.

'Well, let's see if we can make it a deal shorter than you figure on, Whip, you old scalp-hunter, you,' Dallas murmured.

He wheeled the mount, knowing where he was going now. He spurred up a steep incline that had the horse grunting and heaving with back and leg muscles so that he swayed and jerked in the saddle as they passed from level to level. Bushes cracked as they forced a way through, blazing an easily seen trail.

It might throw Whip because of the obvious path but then again the man might be so damn eager to kill that he would ignore any misgivings and plunge on blindly, trigger finger itching beyond endurance. . . .

There was a tower of rocks, some egg-shaped, others standing tall like giant candles or needles. It was right on the top of this mountain – named 'Tower Hill' locally – and there was only one narrow, winding path in and out.

Dallas's mount was panting and snorting as it made its way up in a series of short zigzags. He paused to give it a blow and slipped on his canvas jacket: it was cold up here. *Damn!* There was Whip, impatient as usual, racing his mount, already tired from its fast run out from town, straight at the slope, using quirt and spurs, driving it like a madman, the mount's forelegs scrabbling frantically, close to collapse.

Dallas smiled thinly and turned his own mount towards the last steep section, easing it around the slope now, giving it time to pick its own way. He knew he could be in position long before Whipple showed up on the snaking trail.

Whipple showed up – on foot, leading his staggering mount.

Dallas, above, hidden by two round boulders under the deep afternoon shadow cast by one of the needle rocks, nodded slowly to himself as he watched the so-called deputy, picking his way along the trail. He must know Dallas would have him covered but he showed no fear, only caution.

He was carrying the sawn-off shotgun in his right hand, left pulling the bone-weary mount behind. Dallas lifted his rifle and fired two shots, the canteens kicking wildly and spurting jets of water where they were slung on Whipple's saddle. The horse whiskered and reared, pulling the reins out of the man's hands, lunging away.

Whip dived headlong behind some low rocks, cursing as his heart hammered against his ribs. He crouched in hard, ducking and wincing as two more bullets whined off his shelter, pattering his hunched shoulders with rock chips and dust.

'There goes your water, Whip. That sun'd fry an egg up here in this clear air. You're gonna die a thirsty man.'

'I don't aim to die at all! You're the one gonna do the dyin', Dallas! And I got somethin' special for you.'

'You mean that sawed-off? You'll need to get close to use it properly, Whip. And that'll be too damn close!'

'We'll see! You used your fists to whip me in front of the town. Can't forget that. So I aim to blow your goddamn hands off and let you run around some before I finish you!'

Dallas made a loud *tut-tutting* sound.

'Won't look like a legitimate killing then, Whip!'

'I take you in roped to a hoss, covered with a blanket. They'll only lift the blanket to see who it is. No need for anyone to see you got no hands, 'cept the undertaker – and he's a friend of Tag's.'

'Seems most of the town is. But that won't last much longer. And nor will you!'

Dallas put two more shots in amongst the rocks and Whipple gasped as a rock chip sliced open a three-inch gash along his jawline. He instinctively flung himself back, startled that Dallas could place his lead so well.

Then Dallas stood up, smoking rifle at his shoulder and Whip triggered the shotgun one-handed. Buckshot screamed off the rocks below Dallas and a couple clipped his right leg. He stumbled and missed with his rifleshot and, as he clawed at the rocks, Whipple fired again. The shotgun made its roar of flat thunder and the lead whistled and whined like a bunch of birds with a wildcat in amongst them.

Dallas hit his shoulder hard and dropped the rifle, cursing his own stupidity for showing himself like that.

Who was the impatient one now!

He reached for the rifle, heaved out of the rocks and, ignoring the sting and warm trickles of blood down his right leg, he began thumbing fresh loads through the gate in the side of the rifle's action, half-lying on his back. He heaved down to the sandy patch, twisted around and crawled back, lifting slowly, looking for Whipple.

There was no sign of the man. The deputy's horse was half-way back down the trail and still moving, though slowly, canteens only dripping now.

Where the hell had the man gone. . . ?

Dallas crouched low, hat off, squinting as the sun's low rays glanced off the rocks and into his face as he moved out of the needle rock's long shadow. Was that a little smudge of grey hanging in the air to the left, settling now. . . ? Yeah! Dust. Whipple had gone left, likely looking for a way up and around Dallas's position. Which would mean he would have to appear – *where, damnit?* – Uh-huh, just about – *there!* Barely below his level, but above the end of the snaking trail.

Only other way would be for him to leave the trail, risk clambering over the rocks, many of which were loose and ready to slide if disturbed, and then he would come out *higher* than Dallas. . . .

Dallas didn't much care for *that* and twisted instantly, bringing the rifle around as he looked up.

And saw Whip Whipple's blurred silhouette ten feet above, rising, the sawn-off braced into his hip.

'Close enough, Dallas, you son of a bitch?'

Whip started to chuckle but the sound was drowned in the thunderous crash of gunfire – the shotgun blazing and kicking like a Missouri mule against Whipple's hip, the twin whip-cracks of the rifle almost lost in its roar.

But even as Dallas was hurled back by the slamming power of the buckshot, Whipple reared upright as two rifle bullets drove into him, angling upward under the arch of his ribs, tearing up heart and lungs before bursting out of his back in fist-sized ragged holes that sprayed blood over the rocks, like paint spilled from a pail.

CHAPTER 10

DOWN BUT NOT OUT

It was dark when the Lindons heard the horse in the yard.

Jemma snapped her head up from the sewing in her lap, looking sharply and apprehensively across the deal table at her husband. Corey took his pipe from his mouth, set it on the coffee-can-lid ashtray and stood, going to the wall pegs where the long-barrelled Savage shotgun rested.

'Be careful, Corey.' Jemma spoke in a whisper as he loaded the weapon and, tight-lipped, he nodded, made for the door.

Carelessly, he opened it and stood silhouetted against the lamplight.

'Who's there?'

No answer.

He called again, clearing his throat this time,

handling the shotgun awkwardly. He started when a horse walked into the yellow wedge of lamplight slicing the night.

'God a'mighty, Jem! It's – it's Whipple's mount! The one he rode chasin' Dallas!'

She crossed the room and looked over his shoulder, seeing the bullet-torn canteens, the way the saddle had slipped half-way around the animal's body.

'Is – is he out there in the yard?' she asked hoarsely and Corey tensed.

He hadn't even thought about that! A man not used to danger and the precautions that should be taken, he could have been shot to death minutes ago the way he had exposed himself to an enemy.

But he was lucky. The riderless horse was the only intruder and he soon soothed it, off-saddled, and turned it into the corral. It had already drunk at the trough and there was feed in the corral bin.

'Where's Dallas?' Jemma asked.

Corey was gazing off into the night, in the direction of the hills.

'I – I think I'm goin' to have to go and find out.'

Her hands tightened on his arm.

'Corey. Can't it wait till daylight? You don't know those hills very well.'

'Dallas mentioned Tower Hill, that he could lie for Whipple up there if he could make it in time. There's no blood on the saddle but those canteens have been bullet-shot. Dallas could be lyin' out there, hurt. I don't think I can leave it till mornin', Jem.'

She watched him as he turned back into the cabin,

and reached for his hat and the six-gun in its holster on the bullet belt dangling from a peg behind the door. It was dusty because he had hardly ever used the weapon. He buckled it about his waist awkwardly while she made him up a grubsack.

'I'll put in iodine and some clean cloth you can use as bandages – just in case.'

He hesitated, not wanting to leave her, yet afraid to take her with him. But he knew she should wait at the cabin.

She clung to him, trying to hide the fear she felt about being left alone here at night for the first time since they had settled the JL.

Dallas had been going in and out of consciousness for some time and he slept for a while, found the stars were out when he again opened his eyes.

He was shivering and when he moved he moaned aloud for the pain in the right side of his chest. But the jacket had saved him fatal injury, the heavy canvas and padding having stopped the balls penetrating too deeply. There was sticky blood in several places where the buckshot had raked him.

He turned his head, lifted it stiffly, and saw Whipple's unmoving boots sticking up at an odd angle from the rock line above. Well, he knew his two fast shots from the rifle had gone home and that Whipple was dead, so there was no need to worry about him.

There was just himself now.

How badly was he hit and how much blood had he lost?

He tried to move his body and found that muscles had locked in this cramped position and it was sheer agony to use them. But it would only worsen if he didn't so he set about turning over so he could push against the rocks and work into a proper sitting position. There was a lot of grunting and heavy breathing, much pain which eased some after he managed to get his body out of the cleft it was jammed in. 'Out' was not quite the right word – all he was able to do was take some pressure off but that was a mighty relief.

Sweat soaked him and he felt several balls of buckshot grinding just beneath the skin of his right shoulder and high on that side of his chest. He'd been lucky the shot hadn't penetrated far, but lying for so long, jammed in the rocks, chilled by the night air, his body was stiff and bruised, which caused much of his agony.

He almost cried aloud, getting his arms freed properly. Then he used his left hand to open his shirt, ripping off the buttons. It felt easier, but blood started to flow again over his chilled flesh. It took some time to loosen his neckerchief and he was just wadding it over the small nest of oozing holes in his upper chest when he heard the horse.

Dallas froze, reaching for his rifle, at the same time trying to hitch around so there would be no weight on his six-gun holster. The horse was on the trail below, hoofs clattering a little, the animal giving a snort of fear, on that twisting, dangerous part that was bad enough to negotiate in daylight, let alone at night.

Someone wanted to get up here pretty badly, he decided, rifle in his grip now, working the lever slowly and as quietly as possible. He bared his teeth as even that small movement sent wriggling claws of pain across his chest and up into his neck.

Then he swore.

A voice called hoarsely:

'Dallas? You up there? You OK?'

Judas priest! That crazy damn Lindon! He could get himself killed, giving away his position like that!

'Here!' he called softly. *Might as well now that Lindon had made it clear who he was looking for. Anyway, he didn't think anyone would come looking for Whipple.* 'I'm hit.'

'Where are you? Can't see a damn thing!'

Dallas bit back a curse.

'Just follow the trail. To the base of the needle rocks! And do it *quietly*!'

He tried to ignore the pain as he twisted around and lay half on his side, straining to see. There was enough light for him to make out the thin thread of trail and he soon spotted the rancher, followed him all the way up.

'I could've picked you off a dozen times!' he said when at last Lindon clambered over the rocks to where he lay. 'Don't you know better than to make all that racket? And call out names? Jesus, just calling out at *all* was dangerous!'

Lindon was panting.

'Sorry. My horse was makin' me nervous. I thought it was going to fall several times. Are you hit badly?'

'Might as well light a vesta and see,' Dallas gritted.

'But for Chris'sakes do it down in the cleft just in case there is somebody else alive on this mountain.'

Dallas sweated all the time Lindon worked on him, tense, finger curled around the rifle's trigger, head swivelling.

'Those balls'll have to come out,' Lindon told him. 'I can't do it here – but I think I can stop the bleeding some.'

'Then do that! I don't think anyone will come looking for Whipple till daylight but we better get off this mountain as fast as we can.'

'I – thought we might stay here – just till it got light enough to see the way down. It – it's mighty dangerous.'

'And mighty dangerous to stay put! Patch me up and get me on my horse. We'll find the way down somehow.'

Corey Lindon was far from happy with that.

'Do you – d'you think you should – come back to my place?'

Dallas sighed and even that hurt his chest.

'Don't see I have much choice. But there is a place I used to know – somewhere I could hide and Daybright wouldn't—'

'No, what I meant was – well, you really need a doctor. I could get you into town under cover of night if we move right now, and . . .'

Dallas shook his head.

'No doctor. He might be all right but Tag Daybright seems to have half the damn town in his pocket. Can't risk it, Corey. Look, get me down off this mountain and I'll tell you where to go. If the place isn't there now, well – that's too bad. We'll play it by ear.'

Collecting his things, Lindon paused suddenly, snapping his head around to look at Dallas.

'Are you – talkin' about someplace on that land you used to work?' he asked tightly.

Dallas nodded, watching the man's blurred, pale face, seeing the tightening of the jawline.

'Yeah.'

'But that's – Top D land now!'

'Uh-huh. You know of a better place for me to hole up? A hideout on his land is the last place Daybright's going to look for me.'

'But – you'll be in danger all the time! Someone might see you – figure out you'd pull somethin' like that. . . .'

'Well, they'll sure know they've been in a fight if it works out that way.'

Lindon helped Dallas to his feet, taking a lot of the man's weight as he leaned over to the right in an effort to ease the pain.

'Whatever it is that brought you back to this neck of the woods, Dallas, must be mighty important.'

'That so?' Dallas felt sweat run across his face and trickle down his neck. He was short of breath.

'Yeah, I think that's so. I reckon, wounded and all as you are, you're still thinkin' about whatever it is that's on that land you used to work.'

Dallas didn't answer and Lindon smiled thinly, because, in his book, that was answer enough.

It took most of the cold, dark hours to locate the

hiding-place that Dallas had in mind.

Corey Lindon was mighty nervy as soon as they crossed on to Top D land. Several times he wandered off the trail, Dallas only realizing it after a while because the pain was reaching him now with the movement in the saddle, dulling his senses.

'Keep this up, Corey, and we'll still be travelling come daylight.'

'Sorry. Can't help it. I – know how rough Daybright plays. His men are paid to harass any of us homesteaders and to give us a beating if we're found on his land.'

'That's normal enough. Ranchers and nesters hardly ever get along.'

'And I don't understand that! I mean – *I* don't want trouble. I know Hanrahan doesn't either, nor does Flute or Callum. Yet Daybright's crew go out of their way to harass us in town or on the trail or on our own range even. And Garner always takes Daybright's side.'

'Because he's paid to. And Tag Daybright's smart. He distances himself from his men at such times, so, if there should be any trouble for him, he can say it was their own doing and he'll fire them on the spot. Makes him look good.'

'Sure! Then sets them up proving-up on land adjacent to his and they'll sell out to him in the end!'

'Corey – life ain't hardly ever fair. You gotta get used to that. You might have a hard time of it, but you stand your ground and you'll prove-up all right.'

'Know damn well I will!' Lindon answered with feeling. 'It's – like my only chance to prove to

Jemma's folks, and my own, back in Virginia that I can make my own way in the world.'

'That's all you need. A good strong reason like that. You'll make it, Corey. I just hope we make that hideout before sun-up. . . .'

It was the kind of urging Lindon needed – he was worrying about Jemma being alone all night at the cabin. He paid attention to Dallas's directions and two hours before sun-up they found the place. It was not a cave as Corey had expected. It was no more than a crevice between lightning-splintered boulders but there was a step down and a short steep incline that plunged well below the trail line, deep enough to hide both man and horse.

'You've got no shelter from the weather,' the homesteader said, looking around, feeling the coarse sandy ground, but seeing the wheeling stars above.

'I can cut boughs from that clump of trees back yonder if I need to. Fact, I'll get you to cut me a few leafy ones, jam them against the rocks above me. They'll disperse the smoke if I build a fire, too.'

Lindon shook his head slowly.

'This – this is a dangerous place, Dallas! Someone's only got to look over the edge up there and you'll be a sittin' duck!'

Dallas, propped up now against some rocks, lifted Whipple's sawn-off shotgun. His rifle was lying against his leg and his six-gun was holstered at his waist.

'A duck that shoots back . . . no one'll bother looking. Why would they? There's no indication this place exists, just another crevice.'

'You found it.'

'Chasing a deer I'd wounded, didn't want it to go away and die in agony. It holed up here but I followed the spoor.'

'Could happen again.'

'Aw, go on home to Jemma, Corey! You're the biggest Job's comforter I've ever met.'

Lindon smiled sheepishly.

'I guess I am a worrier—'

'But you'll stick it out.'

'Hell, yeah! I have to.'

Dallas, despite the pain in chest and upper arms, smiled. Whether Lindon knew it or not, he had the makings of a true pioneer.

It was still dark when Lindon eventually rode into the JL ranch yard and hurriedly turned his horse into the corral, taking time only to loosen the cinch strap on the saddle.

He ran towards the house where a light showed at the parlour window, clumped across the porch and called out so as not to alarm Jemma unduly.

'It's okay, Jem. It's only me!'

He opened the door and stepped quickly inside, surprised to see Jemma sitting at the small deal table, looking in his direction, white-faced.

Then a total stranger moved carefully out of the shadows, holding a cocked pistol in his hand, and said:

'Put down that shotgun and come on in, son. We've some palaverin' to do.'

CHAPTER 11

OLD ENEMY

Curly was all flushed and sheened with sweat when he skidded his mount into the Top D yard, bringing Tag Daybright up straight in the cane chair where he sat drinking his after-breakfast coffee and smoking down a cigarillo.

'The hell's your hurry?' he demanded as Curly staggered across, breathless, eyes bulging.

He pointed behind him, arm wavering about.

'Took a look at the Lindon place like you told us to do when we was workin' over that way, boss . . .' He paused and Tag waited, eyes narrowing. Curly gulped. 'Snow lent me his field glasses so I sat on that little ledge under the butte and . . .'

'Judas priest, Curly! *Get to it, man!*'

'Er . . . looked over Lindon's place to see how far they'd gotten with the barn and so on and took one last look in their corrals.' Curly paused again, licking his lips. 'Whip's bronc's there!'

Daybright was on his feet now, cursing as he spilled a little coffee on his striped grey whipcord trousers.

'*Whip*'s horse. . . ? Sure about that?'

'Damn right, boss – not only that, his saddle's hangin' over the top rail and both his canteens have been busted open. Likely by bullets.'

Tag Daybright went very still, thinking of the implications of this.

'No sign of Whip?'

Curly shook his head.

'No. But there's someone with the Lindons. Never seen him but there's a tough-lookin' little grulla pony hitched in the angle of the barn wall they're workin' on. Like it was meant to be out of sight. But me bein' up high, I was able to see it. . . . Ain't no one round these parts I know of with one of them grullas. Usually plainsmen like 'em for long-distance ridin'.'

Daybright knew of no one who owned a grulla either and he had made it his business long ago to keep tabs on who rode what in this neck of the woods.

'You never seen anyone?'

Curly shook his head again. 'Not right then, but ridin' back, just before I went over the ridge, I hipped round in the saddle and seen Lindon saddlin' a couple mounts. I din' want to use the glasses then 'cause the sun was at an angle where it would've flashed off the lenses.'

Daybright looked at Curly sharply: he hadn't realized the man had so many brains. He'd sure never shown evidence of good thinking before this.

'What about Dallas? See him around?'

'Nary a sign. His mount weren't in the corrals far as I could make out.'

Daybright was puzzled. It wasn't shaping up too well. Indications were that Whip had run into trouble – and it had to have come from Dallas, which meant it was *big* trouble. He had to know if Dallas was still alive.

'You didn't stick around to see if Lindon was headed anywhere?'

'He kept lookin' up at the ridge and over towards Top D in general so I stayed outta sight, rode round the ridge and dropped down into the hollow. Just in time to see three riders headin' over the rise towards the creek.'

'Make 'em out?'

'Lindon, his woman – and the stranger, but I couldn't see him too well. He was stayin' close to the woman and it was hard to see much of him. I think he's got a beard.'

'Headin' for the creek. You didn't see 'em cross?'

'Didn't wait that long. Figured you'd want to know. There's somethin' goin' on, boss, and I – well, I sorta got the notion that that stranger was stickin' close to the woman because he was holdin' a gun on her. . . .'

Daybright made his decision.

'Get Frog and Sandy and Hondo – anyone else within holler. Then saddle my buckskin and make sure the rifle scabbard's slung. I'll be down to the corrals in ten minutes.'

Dallas heard them coming and muttered a curse,

moving stiffly around, reaching for his rifle. He had built a small fire and heated the blade of his clasp-knife last night and worked out three of the four buckshot balls from his chest. It hurt like hell but it felt much better now, though his movements were somewhat restricted.

He hoped it wouldn't hinder him if he had to start shooting.

He didn't know who the riders were out there and he stayed put, rifle at the ready, watching the bottom of the cleft for the first sign of company. If whoever it was was headed in towards the cleft, they would have to show soon – and if they didn't look friendly, then they had to be hostile.

And that would be their bad luck.

He saw the top of a hat and started to lift the rifle. His finger was tightening on the trigger when a voice called:

'Dallas? It's me – Lindon.'

'The hell you doing back here?' Dallas didn't lower the rifle and his finger still held the taken-up trigger-slack. He was sure he'd heard more than one horse.

Corey Lindon's head and shoulders appeared and then the man was standing there, afoot. Jemma came up alongside and Dallas tensed. 'Who else is with you?'

'Says he's a friend of yours.'

'I got no friends in this neck of the woods outside of you and Jemma!'

Then Lindon was pulled roughly aside from the narrow entrance. Dallas heard him stumble and swear as his place was taken by a wide-shouldered gent in fringed buckskin jacket, with a wide, flat-brimmed chocolate-brown hat above a grizzled face fringed with silvery whiskers.

The man held a Sharps Big Fifty pointed down at Dallas, with a thumb curled round the big hammer spur.

'Name's Jubal Parry. Mean anythin' to you?'

Dallas frowned, spoke quietly.

'A name I've heard,' he said slowly. 'Long time ago. . . .'

'We met outside Amarillo, 'bout eight year ago.'

'I was never in Amarillo. . . .'

Parry moved awkwardly across the dirt-barred entrance and almost fell as he stepped into the cleft's hidy-hole. Dallas noticed the stiff right leg then and snapped his gaze to the man's face.

'Friend, you're a liar,' Parry said easily. He half-turned to look back. 'Mr and Mrs Lindon, you go hide the hosses, then come on in here. Don't try to run or Dallas'll never leave here alive.'

The Sharps' hammer made a loud ratcheting sound as it was cocked and Jemma, steadied by her husband, looked at Dallas.

'I'm sorry, Dallas. We had no choice but to bring him here. He threatened us. . . .'

Dallas nodded, watching Parry closely.

'Texas Ranger. Retired, last I heard, with a bum hip or leg.'

'You ought to know. You give it to me.'

'Not me. I've never seen you before. Heard your name, but never crossed your trail far as I know.'

Parry spat, rheumy eyes darting now, watching the Lindons as they left to take care of the mounts. He slid his gaze to Dallas who still hadn't lowered his rifle. 'In an old adobe building outside Amarillo. Bunch of you tried to hold up the bank but I got wind of it and moved in. Reckon most of your pards were dead by the time I chased you outta town to them adobe ruins – and you were low on ammo. Trouble is, I miscounted and walked into your last bullet.' Parry touched his right hip. 'Swore I'd catch up with you one day. Yours is the only file I never closed and the damn wound forced me into early retirement. I've had a lot of time to think about you, Dallas. Or "Texas", as you sometimes called yourself way back when—'

'You've got the wrong man, Parry. I've never used "Texas" as a monicker. How many were in this gang that tried to bust the Amarillo bank?'

'You oughta know. But, five as I recollect.'

'Well, I ain't claiming to be any angel, specially right after the War, the time you're talking about, but I rode with no more than two pards, ever. We might've dented the law now and again, and I don't aim to go into details, but we never tried a raid in Amarillo. And we sure never had the Rangers after us. We weren't that big a thorn in anyone's side.'

Parry moved closer, unsteadily, but the yawning barrel of the Sharps swung to keep Dallas covered every second. The Ranger moved so sunlight slanted down on Dallas and the latter pushed his hat back so Parry could get a good look at his battered face, further blurred by stubble.

'Well – I dunno. I only seen you once, close-up. . . .'

'Not me.'

'I only seen this *Texas* close-up once. I never forget a face. His was all dirty and stubbled like yours is now. You're beat-up some, but you could still fit the bill.'

'Parry, I've spent the last eight years or so down in Mexico.'

Parry's watery eyes narrowed and he frowned deeply.

'Well, I heard you might've gone to Mexico.'

'I was there – till about a year ago.'

The old ex-Ranger showed his uncertainty, but it was clear he was thinking hard.

Then he snapped his head up as they heard the sudden clatter of retreating hoofs. Parry made to hitch around towards the cleft's entrance, but his leg wouldn't allow him to hurry and he stumbled – within reach of Dallas's rifle. The Winchester slammed against the Big Fifty and jarred it from Parry's hands. The man staggered and clawed at the rocky wall for support.

Dallas cracked the rifle barrel across Parry's good leg and the man flopped down with a thud and a grunt. He sat there, glaring at Dallas, breathing heavily.

'You son of a bitch!' He tried for the Sharps, straining.

Dallas shook his head.

'Uh-uh. Let the Lindons go. They're just a couple of greenhorns. They ain't in this—'

'They can circle back and gimme trouble!'

'Be of your own making, then. I guess you threat-

126

ened to harm the woman unless Corey brought you here.'

'Well – it was mostly talk. I seen how they were, lovey-dovey, you know – knew he wouldn't risk any harm comin' to her. I wouldn't've hurt her.' Then he sneered. 'Greenhorns or not, they've run out on you!'

'Corey's green but he saw a chance to get his wife to safety and he took it. Which was the right thing to do. He might be loco enough to come back alone, but like I said, forget him.' He paused and then added quietly: 'He brought you to me. You got what you wanted. Let it go at that.'

Parry looked at him sharply, eyes narrowing.

'Damn! You *are* the one gimme this hip at Amarillo, ain't you?'

Dallas sighed.

'It was a long time ago. I was a lot younger and quicker on the trigger then—'

'I knew it! When you went south of the border, you must've been broke, because none of you got away with any money from Amarillo.' The man was relentless, wanted all the details, even at this distance from the actual happening.

'Thanks to you, yeah, I was broke. I'd gotten married by then, started to prove-up on this land, right here where we are now.' That surprised Parry but he didn't say anything. 'Bunch of us tried for some free cattle south of the Rio but ran into trouble . . .' Watching Parry's face, he said quietly, 'Spent the last seven years in *el Inferno Negro*. Heard of it?'

Parry looked mighty sceptical.

127

'The Black Hell? And – you're out and free. . . ?'

'There were six of us decided to make a try at a break-out. Figured we had nothing to lose, knew that likely only one could make it – or maybe no one at all. But anything was better than the *Inferno*. So we made our break and I was the lucky one – if you can call it that. Spent nigh on a year with Injuns before crossing the Rio again.'

'And now you're back – here. Where you started.' Parry said it slowly, thoughtfully. 'I wonder why? Wonder what could have a strong enough pull for you to come back, risk trouble with one of the most powerful ranchers in this part of the State – and work for a couple of greenhorns slap-bang next to where you used to live. I was a Ranger for a long time, Dallas. I might be old and I might've been away from the action for a few years, but there's nothin' wrong with my nose. And I smell somethin' here.'

Dallas simply stared back and Parry smiled crookedly.

'There's somethin' on this land you want, ain't there? Somethin' you come back to get. Risked your neck bustin' outta the *Inferno*, risked trouble with Daybright – and found it – and even when you're wounded you hide out on your old land. Yeah. You've come to get somethin', all right.'

Dallas said nothing for what seemed a long time. He was half-listening for Lindon to come back and try some foolishness – and half considering just how much he should tell this shrewd ex-Ranger.

Hell! The man had been stewing for more than seven years over one desperate bullet, but mostly because he'd had to retire before he could close the file on the outlaws everyone called 'The Tri-State Gang' because they operated in Colorado, New Mexico and Texas. Strictly speaking, only Texas had statehood at that time, the others were still territories, but what was in a name? It was the deeds that counted.

And Parry aimed to close that file now, one way or another, take Dallas in whether he had actual authority or not. . . .

Now there was a dedicated men – or a mighty stubborn one. And a bitter one, to boot. . . .

He had thought he would be able to handle Daybright long enough to get what he came for and slip away. But those two hefty boulders had flung a spoke in the wheels of his high hopes. He was going to need help now.

More help than a greenhorn like Lindon could a give him.

But what if he had read Parry wrong? He might still end up back in jail, or even on the gallows.

Well, maybe he could handle Parry when the time came, too, whatever colours the man showed. But he could use someone tough and experienced like this – and he had taken plenty of risks just to come this far. Hell, he had risked his very life to do it . . . his very life.

He made his decision.

'You ever heard of the *Confederate Eagle Fund*?'

'That stupid legend that started right at the end of the War?'

Dallas shook his head slowly, staring levelly, voice flat and firm.

'It's not just a legend.'

CHAPTER 12

LONE STAR LOOT

Corey Lindon didn't feel good about leaving Dallas with that fierce old ex-Ranger, but his first duty was to Jemma, he reckoned. *He had to get her to safety – then he could start worrying about Dallas – who seemed to be able to pretty much take care of himself anyway . . . .*

Such was Corey's reasoning as he and Jemma made their careful way out of the hills, around the base of the towering rocks. He was sweating and sick to his belly, still hardly able to believe he had been able to thrust Jemma up on to her mount, swing aboard his own and then start them out of that broken country. He had half-expected the Ranger to start shooting, but somehow they had got away with it.

The woman had glanced at him several times, white-faced, but she had looked more puzzled than accusing. In fact, he thought – hoped – the puzzlement was fading into something akin to – admiration.

But he couldn't be sure and this only added to his nervousness.

'We had to grab our chance, Jem!' he said, riding alongside, using his horse on the downslope side to steady her own mount. *A gentleman, a scared gentleman, but one who knew his duty just the same.*

Jemma couldn't help but admire this and she smiled slowly as one word made its way into her mind, unbidden.

Breeding.

She was far from being a snob, but she knew this was what counted, really. Corey was a complex man, part rebel, part loyalist to family tradition. He had rebelled against going into the Lindon family business, just as she had fought against becoming just another useless member of Virginia society when she knew she had talents – and urges – that would be frowned upon by her family.

When she realized Corey had the same traits – and problems – it was a vast relief. And a vast relief for him, too, and so they had run away to the frontier, eyes and heads full of romantic dreams.

Yet the strange thing was that the reality, though vastly different from what either had imagined, was still attractive to them both. They felt as if they were doing something with their lives, *achieving* something. Nothing great, but, in some small way, doing their bit to tame the wild lands. Their efforts would no doubt go completely unnoticed in times to come but they would have that satisfaction themselves of knowing they had accomplished *something* that was important to them both.

Men like Tag Daybright were a worry, even men hard and ruthless like Dallas, but they were both part of this new world after the War, and the challenges had to be met.

She felt herself blush at such thoughts as they made their way down over the broken ground. *She was still a romantic!* But she knew she was trying to take her mind off having run out on Dallas.

Deep down, she knew he could probably handle Parry, although the old Ranger seemed a very hard man, determined to see that his brand of justice was done even after all these years. But once they were down from here they could stop and make some sort of plan to go back and help Dallas.

They really did owe him a lot, although he wouldn't have it that they owed him anything. That was when she had the notion that he was *using* them, as much as he was helping. But he *was* helping in lots of ways and she had figured out that Dallas was the kind of man who would see this as a balance. What he did to help, evened out against whatever it was he was using them for.

She was sure it had something to do with that land he used to work before he came back to these high plains. *This* land, the very land they were riding over now.

'We need to go back home for guns,' Corey said suddenly, startling her out of her thoughts. Parry hadn't allowed them to bring any firearms, of course.

She snapped her head up.

'They might be – gone by the time we get back.'

'Not "we" – just me, Jem. I'm gettin' you out so you'll be safe. We get home, you take the buckboard on into town and wait for me.'

'I can't do that, Corey! I can shoot, you know I can.'

'You can shoot animals for meat, but I don't want you to *have* to shoot at all, Jem! Don't you see that?'

'Well, I'm involved now and I've run out on Dallas just as much as you. We both have to help him, Corey!'

They were in a tricky part on the crumbly edge of a dry wash and neither spoke for some minutes while they worked the horses carefully down, sliding when the dry earth gave way, dust clouds rising. By the time they reached the bottom, they were coughing and half-blinded by the grey fog of dust.

Which was maybe why they didn't see the other riders already in the wash, just coming around a jutting finger of cracked earth, studded with a couple of dozen head-sized rocks.

'Well, now ain't this a surprise!' a voice said abruptly, startling them both. A half-dozen riders came out of the drifting dust.

The Lindons froze in their saddles when they recognized Tag Daybright and a bunch of his hard-cases. Tag was grinning, his face smeared with the dust and grit of a long hard trail.

His clothes were sweat-stained, too, as were his men's, but Tag stood out because, while Jemma and Corey had only ever seen him wearing faded and worn old work-clothes, he had always looked fairly clean. Now he was trail-gritty, though he still had plenty of self-assurance. Now he leaned his hands on his saddle horn, staring hard at the Lindons who were covered by the guns of the Top D crew. He straightened long enough to take a cigarillo from a leather case, fired up, then placed his hands back on the horn. The smoking cigarillo jutted at an angle from his hard mouth as he stared hard at the homesteaders.

'You know you're trepassin'?'

Corey cleared his throat.

'We – got oursleves lost. We were ridin' at night but must've crossed the creek twice without realizin' it. We're just makin' our way back to our own place now.'

Daybright nodded affably enough.

'Risky country to ride in at any time – but plumb loco to do it in the dark.'

'Yes – we – we realize that now.'

'Why the night ride?' Daybright asked as if he was really interested. Corey began to stutter out some stumbling reply but Jemma, looking steadily at the smirking rancher, said:

'Don't bother, Corey. He's playing with you. He knows damn well what we're doing here.'

The fact that his wife used a cuss-word was enough to stop Corey in mid-word and he blinked at Jemma. Daybright touched a hand to his begrimed hatbrim, bowing slightly in Jemma's direction.

'Nice to see one of you has some brains, ma'am. Lindon, we know some stranger rode out with you earlier into these hills . . . and he did a damn fine job

134

of coverin' your tracks. We been lookin' for goddamn hours!' He puffed smoke, eyes slitting as he flicked them from the woman to Corey. 'Dallas is still alive, ain't he?'

Corey frowned, hesitating, and the hesitation was really answer enough. Tag swore softly, then, surprisingly, apologized to Jemma. His voice was hard when he spoke to Corey,

'We know Whip's mount's in your corral, his canteens shot through. My guess is Dallas is wounded, hidin' out somewhere up there. Now, I dunno who this stranger is but he's no greenhorn. You two are gonna take us to him and Dallas – right now.'

'We don't know what you're talkin' about,' Corey said and Tag's temper snapped.

He palmed up his six-gun and fired all in one swift, blurring motion. Jemma screamed as Corey was punched out of the saddle, rolling back over his prancing horse's rump. He hit the dust hard and rolled over, gasping once before lying still, knees half-drawn up.

The men were just as startled as Jemma, and Daybright made no attempt to stop her dismounting swiftly and running to Corey. She looked up, very pale.

'You've shot him in the chest!' Her voice broke and tears welled in her eyes. 'He needs a doctor.'

'Yeah, well, Curly can take him into town – while you show us where Dallas is up there amongst the rocks. We got a deal?'

She swallowed, running a tongue across her lips as

she stared up at him.

'Well, come on! Christ, I've had enough of this.' He jumped off his horse and strode towards her, knocking her hat off with his gun barrel, twisting his fingers in her hair. He yanked her head back painfully and she gasped, eyes afraid.

'It's simple enough, lady,' Tag gritted, thrusting his trail-stained face close to hers. 'Take us to Dallas and your lousy husband has a chance to live! Give me trouble, and . . .'

He thrust out his right hand and placed the barrel against Corey's head, cocking the hammer, watching her coldly.

'Your call. You got three seconds to make it.'

Dallas came back from looking over the cleft's entrance bar, carrying his rifle, but he didn't think Parry was going to give him trouble. Not just now, leastways.

Not till he heard some more about the 'Confederate Eagle Fund'.

Dallas was moving a little stiffly and his head wasn't as clear as he would have liked, but he figured just sitting there propped up against the rock wasn't going to help him recover any faster. He sighed heavily as he sank down again on the flat rock a couple of feet from Parry.

The Ranger held his Sharps Big Fifty across his thighs, loosely, but with thumb close to the hammer spur. He raked Dallas with a bleak stare.

'See anythin'?'

'Lot of broken slope, is all. A trace of dust way

down, but that was likely the Lindons. Figure they'd take their time over country like that out there.'

Parry nodded several times in the way of a man impatient for the other to finish speaking.

'Tell me more about this Confederate Eagle Fund that me and several thousand others always figured was just a rumour started by die-hard Johnny Rebs when they realized they'd lost the War.'

Dallas held his gaze.

'When did you realize we'd lost?'

Parry stiffened.

'We-ell. After Sherman razed Georgia and the Yankees started movin' into the Heartland, I could see we just never had the industrial backin' to keep up the arms and supplies. Hell, most of our boys never even had boots, nor uniforms that fit. We were truly a rag-tag army as Grant called us. . . .' Then his voice hardened. 'But we never thought to surrender! "Let the bastards come!" we used to say. "Remember the Alamo – *Don't Tread On Me!* " Yeah, lot of us realized the South couldn't win but that didn't mean we were gonna lay down our arms and give up. The only way they was gonna take my gun was to pry it from my cold, dead fingers – and I had a lotta friends who vowed the same.'

Dallas nodded.

'Yeah. There was talk about raisin' a secret army in Texas, if there was an armistice, biding time until it was right and then starting up all over again.'

Parry spat.

'Noble sentiments but unrealistic.' Then he frowned. 'Recollect when I was told about it, I asked how such an army was gonna be financed. And that was when I first heard about the "Confederate Eagle Fund".'

'Yeah. Rumours started circulating that the men who still had money in the South, reading the signs, decided not to waste it by just pouring it into arms and supplies from overseas that likely would arrive too late and wouldn't change a damn thing – except to prolong the War and so pile up even more dead. On both sides.'

'I heard them rumours. Some were hard to shake, had the ring of truth about 'em. Or was it just that we had to have some kinda hope and wanted to believe 'em?'

'Reckon that was part of it.'

'But everyone knew even if it was true that there was a fightin' fund supposed to pay for the raisin' of a Texas Army that it couldn't ever happen. The Yankees didn't like Texans and they set out to give us the hardest time of the reconstruction, grindin' us under their boot-heels, keepin' us down. Hell, we're still sufferin' in lots of ways.'

'Light at the end of the tunnel, though,' Dallas pointed out. 'With this land grant getting into full swing and giving us all a chance to make good.'

Parry scowled: he had his own ideas about things.

'Been goin' on too long. But let's get back to this "Eagle Fund". I thought you knew somethin' about it but so far you've told me nothin' I didn't already know.'

Dallas smiled. 'Time to tell you a story—'

'Don't you try your eyewash on me, boy! I know

your background. Why, you told me a passel of lies only an hour ago, denyin' you were the one shot me. . . .'

'You looked like you were gonna blow my head off on the spot if I'd admitted it. Tried to get you calmed down some before I told you it was me.'

'The *Eagle*, damnit!'

'Yeah. I'll start after I left you in that adobe outside Amarillo. . . .'

Parry frowned and Dallas knew he had the man's attention now.

There had been a cold, damp wind blowing out of a skyful of thunderheads all afternoon and night fell early. Loaded down with the wounded Ranger's weapons and leading his horse as a spare, Dallas lit out across the Rio Blanco, and down the Prairie Dog Fork.

He was making for the Indian Territory where he would be beyond any law but federal. And he knew how thinly federal marshals were strung out at that time.

Down on the Red River he ran into Kyle Hanson, a man he had ridden with before and knew from the War. Hanson had a wild bunch with him and they had been hitting the trail herds and hiding out in the Territory. Broke and recovering from a couple of light wounds, it appealed to Dallas and he rode for some months with the Hanson bunch – until the federal marshals banded together and went on a rampage to wipe out the rustlers and outlaws who were thumbing their noses at them across the Red River.

It was one hell of a shoot-out and Dallas was lucky to get out alive. If Hanson hadn't taken him aboard after his horse was shot out from under him, he would have been cut down by the marshals. It was touch and go for several weeks and they ended up hiding out on a small ranch north of San Angelo – friends of Hanson's or kinfolk, he was never quite sure. People named Wallis – the youngest daughter, Carrie, an untouched beauty who seemed to have eyes for Dallas.

He was tempted but figured he oughtn't to repay old Keg Wallis by dallying with the man's daughter and then moving on – as he knew he had to. Law was creeping all over Texas now so he and Hanson cut out to the Llano Estacado, tried their hand at buffalo-hunting and made enough to head closer to the Mexican border which gave them both a feeling of more security. If they had to, they could cross the Rio at full gallop. But Dallas was getting tired of hiding from the law. He changed his nickname from 'Texas' to 'Dallas' – and decided he would like to settle down. Or try to. Hanson was more restless but eventually shrugged grinned, and said: 'Hell! Be somethin' different! Whyn't we give it a go?'

So they did, sold their hides and outfit – but Kyle somehow got them mixed up in a poker-game that ended in gunsmoke with the houseman and his shill dead on the floor, the barman nursing a shattered shoulder, and a sheriff who had been collecting a cut from the crooked games coming through the batwings with a sawn-off shotgun in his hands.

They made it out the back door, stole a couple of

mounts and hightailed it – becoming separated in a rainstorm with a posse closing in. Dallas didn't know what had happened to Hanson, headed south and heard about prove-up land being offered along Comanche Creek.

He rode there – and into an ambush that shot his horse out from under him. He was a long way from Fort Griffin and the deadly poker-game so he hadn't been expecting trouble. But he had his Henry rifle and he spotted the bushwhacker up in the rocks. It took him half an hour to make his way around, get above the man and put his sights on him.

He was surprised to see the man was in uniform, one of the Yankee Reconstruction Army. So he hesitated with his first shot, moved the rifle enough for it to crunch against the sandstone. The Yankee heard the sound, spun on to his back and began shooting, his bullets whining and kicking dust from the rocks all round Dallas. He ducked and weaved his way to the left, threw himself between two boulders when he glimpsed the shooter below and put two bullets into the Yankee.

The man was bad-hit, blood trickling from a corner of his mouth, his chest laid open, uniform bloody, when Dallas walked in on him, smoking rifle cocked and ready to talk again if necessary.

'Damn!' the man gasped as he looked up at Dallas. 'Thought – thought you were – someone else.'

'You killed a damn good hoss – and damn near killed me. You earned what you've got.'

The Yankee surprised him by baring bloody teeth in a grin edged with pain.

'You – you dunno – what I've got, mister!'

'You've got two of my bullets in you and I'd say about a five per cent chance of living.'

That sobered the Yankee some. He nodded gently, coughed bright blood down his already stained uniform jacket. There was some alarm in his eyes now.

'You – you're a – Texan – right?'

Dallas nodded. The man breathed raggedly, making bubbling sounds, coughed up more blood. There was nothing Dallas could do for him – or even had an inclination to do for him. He could call up a thousand reasons why he had no love for Yankees.

A blood-slippery hand grabbed at his wrist and he moved away quickly, alert.

Once again, the wounded man showed that death's head grin.

'*Eagle – Fund*,' he gasped.

Dallas frowned.

'I've heard the rumours. Southern men pouring money into a scheme to roust up a Texas Army. Pipe-dream. It'd cost thousands . . .'

'Hundred – seventeen – thousand – four – four – hunnerd – ninety dollars.'

'What? What're you talking about?'

The man was sinking fast now and he waved one bloody hand, tried to sit up, pointing. Dallas looked around and there, lying in the shadow of the rocks was a long metal box, black and red paint scratched, the remains of what looked like a yellow or golden hawk – maybe an eagle – showing in the centre of the lid. Dallas thought it was a gun-case of some kind.

'That's how much is – in – there,' rasped the Yankee. 'What I – said . . .'

'Money?' Dallas's head was swimming at the thought of so much cash.

The wounded man nodded. 'The *Eagle Fund* . . .'

Dallas felt himself tighten up inside.

'You're joshin'!'

The Yankee had been fumbling at his belt – Dallas had thought he was trying to ease the uniform away from his wound – and pushed a bloody key at the Texan. 'Look . . .'

Dallas did and sat back on his hams, speechless, as the hot Texas sun glinted off gold and silver coins, wads of paper currency. He glanced at the Yankee, saw that grin still plastered there.

'That Confederacy scrip?'

'No. They knew if – ever a Texas Army was – formed – Southern money – would be useless by then. That's US notes. All – spendable. An' – there's a list of – names of the men – who came up with that – cash as well . . .'

'Hell! That part'd be dynamite!'

'It all – is.'

'How come? And how'd you get your hands on it?'

'Long – story. Worked for US Army Intelligence. Lot of persistent – rumours about that fund. Was finally tracked down. Already in the hands of some – Texas – fanatics. Shoot-out. I'm the lone – survivor. Got to figurin' – why take all that – money back – when no one but me – knows it – actually exists?'

'So you were running with it.'

The man nodded, a weary, jerky movement that

required a lot of effort. Dallas knew he wouldn't last much longer.

'Thought you – were on my trail. Sorry.' Then he actually chuckled. 'Neat – twist huh? Now the money – goes to a – a – goddamn Texan – anyway. But – warnin'. Men're still – lookin' – that list can – cause a lot – of trouble. Money is recorded. Coins're Confederate mint – worth their weight in gold or silver. Have to be used – few at a time or – be – some – questions. I was – you – I'd – bury it for a – few years – or – big trouble. Listen, I – gimme a drink, huh. . . ?'

'Sure, Yank. Wish there was more I could do for you.' And Dallas meant that then.

But the man was dead when he got back with the canteen.

Jubal Parry hadn't interrupted Dallas's story once during the telling. Now, when Dallas's pause stretched into a long silence, he said:

'So you buried it on this land?'

'Yeah. Then went and filed on it for prove-up, went back and found Carrie, married her and came back here to make a life for us.'

'Aimin' to dig up your gold later on, huh?'

Dallas nodded.

'Was mighty hard busting a gut, trying to work this damn hard-scrabble land, knowing there was all that money lying within reach. But I wasn't game to touch it and when Hanson, who'd come down by that time, asked me to go along with him and some others to Mexico to rustle steers from one of the big old *ranchos*, I couldn't refuse. I had to appear as hard up as the rest of 'em. But that sure backfired. . . .'

'And now you're back to collect. Which makes me wonder why you ain't done just that.'

Dallas smiled bitterly.

'I buried that Yankee right in that clump of boulders, first sinking the chest of gold deep in the bottom of the grave, then laid him in and covered it up. Figured the rocks would be landmark enough. But they had a flash flood last year and the water moved the boulders, left a couple of mighty hefty ones right smack on top of the grave. I can't move 'em. And dynamite'll blow everything to hell.'

Parry laughed, slapping a hand to his knee.

'Well, if that don't beat all! So you need a hand, huh?'

'Looks like I can't do it alone.'

'Well, I'm your man. And I take you back as well as that *Eagle* gold, they'll give me the biggest pension ever. My name'll go on the Ranger Honour Board . . . For ever!'

As he finished speaking, he swung the heavy Sharps in Dallas's direction and cocked the hammer.

CHAPTER 13

BACK TO YESTERDAY

Dallas smiled thinly.

'I could call your bluff on this, Parry. Then you'd never locate the grave.'

'Hell, you've given me enough so I could find it easy.'

'Hope you're feeling strong. Those boulders weigh about two ton apiece, is my guess.'

Parry pursed his lips.

'Well, that might be a leetle problem. . . .'

'And don't forget you're on Tag Daybright's land.'

Parry sobered now.

'Yeah. I've been hearin' about him. Garner seemed leery of him.'

'On Daybright's payroll.'

'I wouldn't worry too much about Garner. He looks after Garner and no one else. He might take

Daybright's money but he'll step down off the fence on the side that'll do him the most good. So forget him. Let's you and me dicker some more and work things out to our mutual advantage.'

'Way I see it, we work together – likely have to tunnel in under that grave, but I've had experience at tunneling.' At Parry's quizzical look, Dallas added, 'In the Black Hell. We dug our way out.'

Parry shook his head with a touch of admiration.

'If that story's true, you're even tougher than I thought.'

'It's true. Now what I figure we can do is . . .'

He broke off suddenly at the sound of a woman's high-pitched scream.

Parry jumped and the Sharps wavered and Dallas grabbed his Winchester. But both men were looking towards the cleft's entrance as, on the tail-end of the scream was tagged a warning cry:

'Watch out, Dallas!'

They heard horses then and a low sound that might have been men cursing. Then suddenly guns began firing from *above*, the bullets raking their shelter.

'Watch the entrance!' Dallas snapped at Parry, rolling away so he was closer to some rocks that would afford at least a little cover from above.

There were two men up there. They must have clambered up the rocks from the far side so they could see down into this place. Which meant someone who knew about it had told them where Dallas and Parry were.

It had been Jemma Lindon's voice that had called

the warning – and likely made the scream, too. Which meant she was in trouble. . . .

A bullet gouged a line of rockdust and he snapped his head back, blinking, glimpsed the shooter leaning over the edge of a rock up there and got off a fast shot. He heard the bullet ricochet, edging along his line of protecting rocks even as he levered in a fresh shell.

Parry's Big Fifty boomed, the thunder slapping at their ears in this confined space. Dallas looked up in time to see a man literally blown off his feet as he tried to clamber over the entrance bar. The old Ranger reloaded swiftly. Dallas spun on to his back as the man above leaned out for another shot, fired three times, the sounds of the shots blending into one long roar.

The man's upper body was obscured by rock dust and Dallas thought he had missed. Then a rifle clattered down into the rocks and a limp body followed. It struck hard and he heard bones crack as Parry swore and pushed a twisted leg away from him. The dead man slid down into a gap in the rocks. It was Frog, bandages still around his head, askew now.

'Judas! Give a man some warnin', can't you? He nearly landed on top of me!'

Dallas lifted his rifle and triggered as he saw movement up there. A hat flew into space and drifted down towards them. A man swore, ducked back even as Dallas's next bullet sent rock chips flying.

Parry's Sharps boomed again and the sound of the ricochet was like a hundred hornets, apparently striking another rock, then making a higher-pitched sound as it faded away somewhere beyond the cleft.

'Dallas!'

That was Tag Daybright's voice, out there below the entrance.

'Give it up! We've got you cornered.'

Just then Dallas spotted the man above again and he emptied the rifle, dropping flat when the last shell-case spun from the ejector port. But not before he caught a flash of the man rearing back, throwing away his gun in reflex action as lead hammered him down. He fell forward, both arms dangling over the edge, his hair all bloody.

'Hope you brought plenty of men with you, Tag!' Dallas called, reloading swiftly. 'You're losing 'em like they got the plague!'

Parry looked at him sharply and then Daybright called:

'I brought enough – but I brought somethin' else, too. Maybe better'n my crew—' There was silence and then a woman screamed. As it trailed away, Daybright chuckled. 'Hear that, Dallas? You know who it is. She's right here beside me – and my gun's rammed hard into her ribs. You tell him, lady!'

'Dallas!' It sounded more like a breathless gasp than anything else. 'He's – telling the truth!' Jemma sobbed.

After a pause, Dallas asked: 'Where's Corey?'

'He – Daybright shot him! He sent Curly to take him in to a doctor – if I agreed to bring him – here. I'm sorry.'

'You had no choice, Jemma,' Dallas called back,

looking thoughtfully at Parry. 'What d'you want, Tag?'

'You – and that old sidewinder with you. Put down your guns and stand up. I've got a man up above who can see you.'

Dallas looked up quickly: he hadn't seen the third man up there. But, there he was, the one he thought was called Hondo, part-Apache he claimed, holding a long-barrelled Greener so that it covered both men below.

Dallas turned his gaze to Parry. 'He's holding all the cards.'

'Like hell! We put down our guns, we're dead men!'

'And if we don't set 'em down, Jemma's dead.'

'Ah, he won't kill her. Loses the advantage if he does that.'

Dallas shook his head.

'He's using her to do this easy. If he calls our bluff and kills her, all he has to do is keep us pinned down till more men arrive and then shoot us to pieces.'

Parry tightened his grip on the Sharps.

'Why don't we make him do that then? More time we've got, more chance we have of figurin' a way out.'

Dallas narrowed his eyes.

'I heard you were a hard bastard.'

'Heard the same about you – but seems it was wrong. You're soft as hot custard.'

They both tensed as Jemma screamed again, longer this time. She was crying when the scream ended and she called between sobs:

'Dallas! Oh, I'm so – sorry. But – please! I – I'm hurting . . .'

'And she'll hurt a damn sight more if those guns ain't on the ground in five seconds and you come out with your hands up!' the rancher yelled, sounding angry now.

Dallas knew Daybright meant it and he slowly set down his Winchester, glancing up at Hondo and raising his hands to make sure the man realized that he was obeying the rancher's orders.

'C'mon, old-timer!' Hondo called down. 'Not that I mind blowin' your head off . . . but get a damn move on!'

Parry's mouth was tight. He glared at Dallas as he lowered the Sharps' hammer and began to set it down amongst the rocks, speaking quietly.

'Other thing I heard about you was that you're half-brother to greased lightnin' on the draw. . . .' He flicked his eyes meaningfully upwards towards the rim where Hondo stood. He added even more quietly: 'We're like fish in a barrel. And Daybright's got no use for either one of us now!'

Dallas knew he was right, hesitated, thinking of Jemma, but . . .

His Peacemaker came up blazing, his left hand chopping at the hammer, bullets flying around the rocks at Hondo's feet. The man screamed as lead shattered his lower left leg and it buckled under him. The bullets were lifting as the edge of Dallas's hand chopped at the hammer. One took Hondo in the belly, the next just under the arch of the ribs. The man was dancing like a medicine-show puppet, his strings pulled by a madman.

The shotgun thundered and leapt from his hands in recoil, even as Hondo collapsed, one bloody leg dangling over the rim, the other doubled under him.

Then a bullet whined off the rock in front of Dallas and he reared back, stumbled and fell.

Tag Daybright was standing on the entrance bar, holding the wet-eyed woman. Her dress had been ripped off one shoulder and even in that brief glimpse, Dallas saw the cigarillo burns on the top of the half-exposed breast.

Tag, teeth bared, aimed carefully at Dallas. His finger tightened on the trigger and suddenly Parry said:

'Waylon Blackman! By hell, we thought you were dead years ago!'

Daybright tensed visibly at the Ranger's words, held his fire, shifted his gaze to Parry.

'And I heard *you'd* retired a damn cripple! Christ, of all the luck for you to turn up now!'

Dallas watched as Parry spoke again, not taking his eyes off Daybright.

'This man's been a wanted outlaw since just before the end of the War. Led a bunch of hard-ass murderers into some towns, posin' as real soldiers, and wiped 'em off the map in the name of the Confederacy, looted everythin' valuable – killed everyone, women, kids, oldsters. There was no one left to fight for the town. All the young men were either away at the War or had been killed by it.'

'Led you a merry dance, Parry!' Daybright sneered.

'Killin' off your men one by one, finally fakin' your own death!'

Daybright shrugged, recovering from his first shock now.

'Grew a beard to change my appearance, but couldn't stand it in this Texas heat. Knew I was takin' a chance shavin' it off but never expected to run into anyone who'd known me from that other time. No matter, though. You're goin' into permanent retirement right now, Parry!'

'No wonder you were fussed about any law coming down here after me or to investigate complaints from the homesteaders,' Dallas said, getting Daybright's attention. 'You knew if that happened, you might be recognized, but in any case there'd be trouble enough to stop you building the dam . . . which you need to take control of the high plains.'

Daybright laughed harshly.

'Well, nothin' to stop me now, is there? You two are gonna die where you stand and the woman might as well die along with you. I'll arrange things so one of you gets the blame. . . .'

'No!'

The voice came from beyond the cleft and Daybright spun quickly. The girl was quick-witted enough to pull away. The rancher staggered and then a six-gun roared and he was blown down into the cleft by the first strike of lead, the second and third wrenching his body violently. But he was already dead before he struck the ground.

Jemma had fallen when she had pulled away, quickly scrambled to her feet and cried: 'Corey!'

Dallas scooped up his rifle and was moving fast, ignoring the tightening in his chest as he felt a little blood start to ooze from his wounds. He jumped on to the entrance bar and saw Jemma holding tightly to Corey Lindon who was sinking to the ground, a smoking pistol in his hand.

'Lend a hand here, Parry!' Dallas called as he climbed down and knelt beside the wounded home-steader. Jemma was covering Corey Lindon's dirt-smeared face with kisses and tears of joy.

The man looked past her spilling hair and gave Dallas a wan smile.

'My pipe in my pocket deflected the bullet a little,' he gasped. 'Not much more'n a gouge across my chest. Curly wasn't very good at watchin' me, figured I was no danger. But I managed to push him off his horse and he hit his head on a rock. I – think he'll be all right, though.'

'Nothing for you to worry about,' Dallas said. 'You saved our necks, Corey.'

Lindon smiled tentatively as Jemma began to examine his chest wound.

'I – I was still scared.'

'Friend, so was I,' admitted Dallas.

Parry predicted that, once word got out that Tag Daybright was dead, his men, all hardcases, hired at fighting wages and so owing no allegiance except to the dollar, would loot the Top D of whatever they could take and then head out.

This was what happened: they even burned the ranch house. Otis Garner stayed well back and

154

allowed it to happen. Officially, he would claim he didn't know anything about it until it was all over and done with.

And he made it plain he didn't *want* to know about anything that Dallas and that hard-nosed Texas Ranger were getting up to. From now on, he was sticking to his job: sheriff of Comanche Creek, taking the town council's pay, showing no favourites, just a conscientious small-town sheriff.

But Parry had plans to see that word would reach the right authorities about Garner's earlier corruption. For now, though, he was busy with other things.

Corey Lindon's chest wound wasn't as bad as he had thought – in fact, the shock having knocked him cold when it happened had likely saved his life. If Daybright had figured it was only a flesh wound, he would have shot him again, this time fatally.

But he couldn't do much to help Parry and Dallas as they began to tunnel under the grave of the unknown Yankee.

Dallas's chest hurt some and bled a little but the buckshot wounds were not deep and, anyway, there was a lot of silt left by the flash flood so it was not as if they had to dig through the hard-packed earth all the way.

They had started the tunnel ten feet out from the grave where the huge boulders rested. If their weight still collapsed the grave, the men would have a chance of getting out of it alive. Once through the top layer of silt, of course, they reached the hard-packed original ground and progress slowed some.

Parry was a tough old codger but he had a lot of

years packed into that raw-boned frame and there were limits to his efforts. His stiff right leg was of some advantage when he crawled into the tunnel to shovel out the dirt and blocks of soil Dallas had loosened, but mostly it was mighty awkward and he expended much energy just cursing the pain and cramping muscles as he twisted this way and that.

'I just hope,' he gasped during one of the rest periods, 'that the damn flood didn't wash the whole kit-and-kaboodle away!'

'No – I'm sure I found the grave all right,' Dallas assured him. 'It had sunk in some, with time, but it's there.'

'Better be – after all this!'

Dallas looked hard at the man: he still wasn't sure what was going to happen if – when – they did find the steel box. He was prepared to fight Parry if he had to, but he hoped it wouldn't come to that.

Dallas had come too far to give up now.

They broke through on the second day, just after high noon.

Dallas was in the tunnel, breathing hard, sweating gallons in the heat, the air thick with dust – and another underlying smell that was familiar from all those years of the War – the smell when you first marched on to a battlefield a few days old. . . .

He worked with a neckerchief tied over the lower half of his face, coughing a lot, lungs filling with dust.

He drove the pick-axe into the earth, gouged out a lump, laboriously worked it down and around behind him, then swung the pick again in the restricted space.

There was a dull *clunk*!

He froze. Then he moved the pick back and forth, up and down. His ears were filled with a lot of loose dirt but he heard the sound clearly enough – a dull kind of screech.

Metal on metal.

He backed out, Parry on the way in to get the loosened dirt swearing at him, telling him his shift at digging was not yet an an end.

'Think – it – is,' gasped Dallas as he slithered out into daylight. Jemma and Corey Lindon were watching tensely as he lowered his neckerchief, wiped grit out of his eyes. 'I think I just hit metal. But there's a bit of dirt trickling down. Maybe from the weight of the boulder. Be best if we shore it up before . . .'

Parry was back in the tunnel faster than they had ever seen him move before. They heard him scraping away and cursing and after twenty minutes he backed out, pulling a dirt-caked, rusted long iron box.

'Look out!' Corey yelled. 'The rock's movin'!'

It was the biggest boulder, closest to the end of the grave where they had been tunnelling. It creaked and shifted with a thud, as if that end of the tunnel had collapsed under the weight. Dirt shot into the air and a choking gust blasted out of the tunnel mouth as they ran to get clear.

The rock swayed and then began to roll along the line of the tunnel, collapsing it with its weight. Jemma and Corey were well clear but Parry's game leg hindered him, plus the weight of the chest. Dallas grabbed him under the arms and literally threw him out of the way as the huge boulder thumped and

157

bounced past not a yard away. It continued on down the slope, flattening bushes and the ground itself before splashing into the creek and bringing up finally against the opposite bank.

The four people sat where they were staring, unable to speak right away.

Then Parry staggered to his feet, grabbed the upended chest where it had fallen and set it on its base, panting. He spat.

'Smells like a grave in there! Pick got caught up in a couple bones, too, and maybe loosened . . .' He caught the look on Jemma's face and the warning glance from Corey, and shut up, turning his attention to the box.

It was not in good shape, not after so long in the ground. But while there was a good deal of rust, nothing had actually collapsed. They looked at each other. Dallas lifted the pick and began to work on the lid. He had long ago lost the key. And when at last the lid creaked up, they stared dumbfounded at the pile of glittering gold and silver coins, looking as if they had just been minted. The bundles of paper currency hadn't fared so well. Many of them were rotted and crumbling, likely from build-up of moisture inside the box over the long burial underground. A piece of paper that had once been folded with writing on it – like a list of names – crumbled to dust when Parry picked it up.

'Best thing that could've happened,' he murmured. 'Now – that money has to be counted,' Parry said officiously and they were surprised to see he had his six-gun in his hand. 'And counted accurately. Just use the notes that aren't damaged. C'mon, get movin', folks. I want to know how much is left before I send in my report.'

No one said anything. Dallas shovelled out three piles of coins, looking coldly at the Ranger, and he and Jemma and Corey began counting.

With the notes that Parry figured could still be used as legal tender, the total came to a little more than a hundred thousand dollars.

They sat back, still stunned at the sight of so much money. Parry was still covering them with his six-gun and he awkwardly made a note of the amount in his small notebook.

'You turning it over to the government?' Dallas asked tightly.

Parry held his gaze, looked at Jemma and Corey.

'Rightfully theirs.' After a silence he said: 'Nice round figure, a hundred thousand. Forget the odd dollars over and above that – Comanche Creek can use an infirmary and that extra money can get one started. But a hundred thousand – kind of awkward to divide evenly into three, ain't it?'

Jemma's mouth sagged. Corey blinked. Dallas's face didn't alter.

'Three,' he said.

Parry nodded. 'One third to you for findin' it – a third to the Lindons for their help – a third to me.' He smiled crookedly. 'My pension pay-out. Kind of a record, I guess, but – well, reckon I've earned it!'

Dallas was silent for a time; then he smiled.

'I reckon you have. . . .'

He thrust out his hand and Parry hesitated, then

gripped with him, jerking his head to where Jemma was clutching tightly to the stunned Corey Lindon, both smiling.

'Ain't made too many folk happy in my life, but reckon I've done it this time. And I wouldn't be here at all if you hadn't hauled me outta the way of that runaway boulder.'

'Wanted to see what was in the chest,' Dallas said, by way of dismissing Parry's attempt at thanking him. 'Where you headed?'

'Back south-west of Fort Worth, I guess. I've just been rentin' that small spread up there. Me an' the wife both like it. Reckon I might buy it now. That's what I'm gonna do, and we know what the Lindons are gonna do with their share, but what about you, Dallas?'

He thought for a spell then said, sighing:

'Reckon I might take a ride back to yesterday.'

They stared at him blankly.

'Still got a wife up in New Mexico who don't exactly hate me. We got about seven or eight years of yesterdays to make up for.'

They all figured that was a damn good idea.